LOUISE'S BLUNDER

LOUISE'S BLUNDER

Sarah R. Shaber

This first world edition published 2014
in Great Britain and the USA by
SEVERN HOUSE PUBLISHERS LTD of
19 Cedar Road, Sutton, Surrey, England, SM2 5DA.

Trade paperback edition first published 2017
In Great Britain and the USA by
SEVERN HOUSE PUBLISHERS LTD

British Library Cataloguing in Publication Data
A CIP catalogue record for this title is available from the British Library.

ISBN-13: 978-0-7278-8392-6 (cased)
ISBN-13: 978-1-84751-789-0 (trade paper)
ISBN-13: 978-1-78010-558-1 (e-book)

In honor of Fosse, my family's miniature schnauzer, my constant companion for almost fourteen years. Good dog!

ACKNOWLEDGEMENTS

It's true that writing is a solitary occupation, but it takes a small army to support a writer and get a manuscript turned into a book. As always I must thank my family, my husband Steve, my daughter Katie and my son Sam, for putting up with me while my creative juices are flowing.

My writing buddies, Margaret Maron, Bren Witchger (Brynn Bonner), Diane Chamberlain, Kathy Trochek (Mary Kay Andrews), Katy Munger and Alexandra Sokoloff, I can't imagine my writing life without you!

My friend Vicky Bijur is the best agent in the universe.

I am so fortunate that Quail Ridge Books in Raleigh is my home bookstore.

And I am very thankful that Severn House publishers took a chance on this series during the depths of the recession. To my editor, Rachel Simpson Hutchens, thank you for your patience!

ONE

The following is an excerpt from the '1943 Guide to Hiring Women', published in the July 1943 issue of Mass Transportation *magazine. It was written for male supervisors of women in the workforce during World War II.*

Pick young married women. They [. . .] usually have more of a sense of responsibility than do their unmarried sisters; they're less likely to be flirtatious; they need the work or they wouldn't be doing it [. . .]; they still have the pep and interest to work hard and to deal with the public efficiently.

The GI ground his cigarette butt into the heap of decaying cherry tree blossoms. Just the color, a rotting baby girl pink, made him angry. What was he going to tell his children and grandchildren? That he spent the war guarding three thousand lousy Jap bushes? If it were up to him he'd have every one of them uprooted and burned in the biggest bonfire Washington DC had ever seen.

After Pearl Harbor four of the cherry trees had been vandalized. Since then, on orders from the Great Father himself, regular Army soldiers had been stationed around the Tidal Basin to protect the remaining trees. Which were now called 'oriental' trees. Which didn't fool anyone. Imagine, the US Army guarding a grove of pink trees! It was embarrassing, that's what it was. He lied in his letters home, telling his dad that he was learning to operate an M3 Light Tank. If the old man found out the truth he'd never hear the end of it.

The soldier gazed out over the shimmering blue water of the Tidal Basin. He had to admit it was a pretty sight, especially on a soft May early morning like this one. The circle of cherry trees, now fully leafed out, framed the gleaming white marble of the new Jefferson Memorial to the south. If he turned and looked north, he'd see the Washington Monument standing tall, keeping watch over the District. And at midday the grassy banks of the Tidal Basin would be crowded with pretty government girls eating their sandwiches.

But he wasn't fighting the Nazis. Nightly he prayed, silently so his bunkmates couldn't hear him, that when the United States invaded Europe, which had to happen someday, he'd be in the ranks of fighting men sent overseas. It was what he wanted more than anything else in the world. Just thinking about being stuck in the States for the entire war made him want to heave.

Something drifting in the Tidal Basin floated into his field of vision. He squinted, cupping his hands over his eyes to block the sun. Whatever it was bobbed toward the shore – the tide was coming in. The object rolled over and he saw a face. Jesus Christ!

The young GI turned and shouted out to the sentry closest to him.

'Help!' he screamed. 'Help! Man overboard!' He pointed out into the water. At ten feet deep the Tidal Basin was plenty deep enough to drown in.

The soldier flung his rifle to the ground, threw off his helmet and dropped his duty belt. He unlaced his boots in record time and plunged into the cold water. Within a few feet the water deepened and he started swimming. It wasn't like swimming in the lake at home; it was slow going against the tide. He could hear shouting from behind him on the shore.

By the time the soldier reached the body he knew the fellow was dead. Just the way the body rolled in the small swells told him that. And the color of the man's face confirmed it. Nonetheless he grasped the corpse under its arms and began to tow it back to shore. The dead weight of the body slowed his progress to what seemed like nothing, but then another soldier joined him and the two of them dragged the dead weight of the corpse to shallow water quickly. Another GI waded out and helped them lug the waterlogged corpse to land.

His squadron leader, Sergeant Tyson, stood on the shore barking into his radio. He clicked it off and nodded to the young soldier.

'Good work spotting that guy,' Tyson said. 'I've called the District police. A patrolman will here soon. And a mortuary wagon.'

The four soldiers, three of them dripping wet, stared down at the corpse, splayed face up on the grass.

'He hasn't been dead long, I'd say,' Tyson said. 'Not much bloating.'

The victim was not a young man, maybe forty, dressed in civvies – khaki trousers, a white short-sleeve shirt and brown wingtips. A ballpoint pen stamped 'US Government' was clipped to his shirt pocket. It had leaked ink all over the front of his shirt.

'Guy's just a pencil-pusher,' the sergeant said. 'Wonder how he got himself drowned.'

A teetering stack of intelligence reports jammed my in-box. It was my job to analyze them and then to summarize them on index cards. The cards would be added to our vast index card files and the documents themselves filed in one of the hundreds of file cabinets that crowded the Central Information Division, or Registry, of the Office of Strategic Services, our country's wartime spy agency. So that other OSS divisions, the Army and Navy, the State Department and the White House, had access to the latest intelligence.

This was a critically important job for which I and the other forty or so girls who worked in the Registry (secretaries of war, ha-ha; boy, had that joke gotten old) were well paid – for females, that is. But the interminable task was wearing me out. It wasn't unusual for some general bristling with chest hardware to hover over me, stone-faced and arms crossed, while I analyzed a document he wanted yesterday. Or for some irreplaceable file to go missing, only to be found after hours of

searching, forgotten on some analyst's desk. And at the end
of the workday every file that had been left on the return
table in the OSS Reading Room had to be replaced in its
original location before the next day. At least the record cold
and ice-bound winter of 1943 was over and I could walk home
in the twilight of a warm spring evening.

What I wouldn't give for a transfer! I'd heard the librarian
of the Registry's telephone book archive had left. Even that
job sounded good to me.

I turned when I felt a gentle tap on my shoulder. Pat, one
of our Negro messengers, stood behind me.

'Mrs Pearlie,' he said. 'Mr Wilmarth Lewis requests your
presence in his office right away.'

My stomach lurched. Lewis was the Chief of the Central
Information Division. A famous Walpole scholar from Yale,
he'd invented the indexing and cross-indexing system that kept
our Registry's millions of index cards, thousands of foreign
serials, fifty thousand books, the Map Room and countless
loose postcards catalogued so that they could be located by
the researchers who needed them. But Lewis was an aristocrat
and dandy who didn't bother with the day-to-day running of
the Registry. He spent his time with people like OSS Director
General Bill Donovan and Archibald MacLeish, the Librarian
of Congress. What on earth did he want with me? I couldn't
imagine he even knew my name. I had done some fieldwork
in the past, and although my participation was both accidental
and controversial, I had acquitted myself very well. But I
doubted very much that Lewis knew anything about my
fieldwork.

The messenger had left when I realized I had no idea where
Lewis's office was. I caught up with him between the row of
file cabinets where 'Q' ended and 'R' began. The young
colored man grinned at me. 'You mean you don't know your
way around the main building? Mr Lewis's office is on the
same hall as General Donovan's. Right next to the water
fountain.'

*   *   *

Lewis's secretary occupied a desk outside his office in a wide hall on the upper floor of the main OSS building, which had once been a naval hospital. She directed me to wait in a nearby chair. Then she went back to typing from her shorthand notebook, mouthing words to herself as she typed. I barely had time to compose myself and apply a little face powder and lipstick before her telephone buzzed and she indicated that I was to go into Lewis's office.

I knew Lewis was wealthy – he was funding the Yale Walpole Library himself. But I'd never seen an office at OSS like this one. An oriental carpet covered the floor and the desk was a walnut leviathan inlaid with some lovely golden wood I couldn't name. Two leather club chairs faced the desk. Obviously Lewis had furnished the office at his personal expense.

Lewis stood behind his desk with his fingers resting on a thick file. My personnel file! I could clearly see my name on the tab. My pulse pounded in my head and I felt drops of perspiration form behind my neck.

'Mrs Pearlie,' Lewis said. 'Please have a seat.'

I took one of the deep leather chairs. Lewis remained standing and glanced down at my file before raising his eyes to my face again.

'For a government girl you have quite a record,' he said. 'Superior commendations, Top Secret clearance. You haven't spent your time with us just filing and typing, have you?'

'No sir,' I said, dry-mouthed.

Lewis tucked a hand into his pants pocket, revealing a heavy gold watch chain with a Phi Beta Kappa key dangling from it.

'We need you to do something for us today. It's rather distasteful.' The man wrinkled his nose as if he'd smelled something nasty. 'My secretary is going to the cafeteria for coffee and I'm required at a meeting. You'll be joined shortly by an officer with the OSS Security Office. You're to work for him and report only to him, am I clear?'

'Yes, sir,' I said. What on earth was this about?

*   *   *

Several long minutes later the office door opened and a man entered whom I would have been hard-pressed to identify as a security officer. He was wearing an Army major's uniform that hadn't spent any time with an iron lately. His top shirt button was undone and his tie loosened. He was shorter than I and weighed, I would guess, fifty pounds more. We shook hands. 'Mrs Louise Pearlie?' he said. 'I'm Major Angus Wicker, OSS Security. Good to meet you. I understand you can keep a secret.'

'Yes, sir, I can,' I said. Now I was intrigued.

He sat down in the other leather chair and crossed his legs. His uniform jacket fell open and I saw a handgun holstered at his side. He wore a hefty gold class ring on his right hand. I'd learned at The Farm, the OSS training facility, how much damage a heavy ring could cause in hand-to-hand combat. Maybe Lt Wicker was more capable than he appeared.

'I have an assignment for you, Mrs Pearlie. And I must tell you that it comes from the very highest levels of OSS. Top Secret, Eyes Only and all that.'

'I'm ready.' Was I ever!

'Do you know a Research and Analysis staffer named Paul Hughes?' he asked. 'Thin, fortyish, sandy hair, Europe/Africa division?'

'The name is familiar but I can't place him,' I said.

'He's an economist on the German desk, specializes in German labor statistics. We need you to find out what files he's been checking out in the Reading Room over the past month. He's not in today, so now would be a good time.'

'All the files?' I said.

'Just the regular files,' he said. 'Hughes doesn't have access to the Limited files. And we need specifics. Give us the file numbers and subject titles. Mr Lewis has told Mr Shera that you'll be compiling statistics for him today.' Shera was the Head of the Reference Section, my boss. 'At the end of the day place your notes in an envelope, seal it and sign across the seal. Bring it back to this office and observe Mr Lewis place it in his safe. That's all.'

'What if I'm not finished?'

'Add a note to that effect. We'll take it from there.'

'All right.'

'And Mrs Pearlie, you might not hear anything about this ever again.'

'I understand.'

I practically ran back to the huge old apartment building across the street that housed the R&A Branch and the Registry. OK, it was just one day free from my regular job, and I'd still be doing clerical work, but by God, I was looking for a double agent! Well, perhaps it was wrong to use such a strong term. But Hughes was reading files that he shouldn't be reading; why else would he do that except to share the information with someone he shouldn't? That was the only reason I could think of why the big OSS bosses wanted to know what files this Paul Hughes checked out! Even better, I'd been trusted to do the job.

District Police Detective Sergeant Harvey Royal slammed the door of the old black Chevy police car and cased the accident scene. A motorcycle policeman stood guard over a soggy corpse splayed across the path that circled the Tidal Basin. His motorcycle leaned up against the nearest cherry tree. A mortuary van with its rear doors opened wide was parked on the grass nearby, its white-clad driver and his assistant leaning up against the vehicle, smoking. An Army sergeant supervised a handful of soldiers who were preventing a gathering crowd from getting a good look at the corpse. Royal walked with a limp over to the motorcycle policeman and the body.

'What the hell, patrolman?' Royal said. 'You'd better have a good reason to call me to the scene of a drowning. This stiff should be on its way to the morgue by now.'

The patrolman removed his helmet revealing a young freckled face and a ginger cowlick.

'Sir,' he said. 'The victim had no identification on him. No wallet, nothing in his pockets at all. Only that government pen clipped to his shirt pocket. And he's got a big old lump behind his right ear, too.'

'No kidding,' Royal said. He knelt clumsily next to the corpse and turned out all the victim's pockets. 'No wallet,' he said to himself, 'no cigarettes, no lighter, no handkerchief, no pocketknife, no keys. Nothing.'

Royal bent over the corpse and felt around the back of its head. There was a lump behind the right ear, all right. A big one. He felt a depression in the man's skull beneath the lump. Royal got to his feet and wiped his hands with a handkerchief he pulled from his pocket. He nodded in approval at the young patrolman. 'You did the right thing to call me, son. Go on and radio for a photographer.'

'You mean he didn't drown?' the Army sergeant asked. He'd been hovering nearby, after sending his soaking wet soldiers back to their barracks to change into dry clothes and ordering the rest of his squad to contain the civilians that gathered on the bank of the Tidal Basin to gawk at the corpse.

'I don't know,' Royal said. 'It's unusual for a fellow not to have a wallet or anything else in his pockets. Makes me wonder if someone didn't empty them out for him. Help me turn him over.'

Royal and Sergeant Tyson rolled the corpse face down and Royal folded back the victim's shirt collar. 'No laundry label,' he said. He grabbed the victim's belt and pulled his trousers down, and underwear with them. The crowd murmured disapprovingly. Royal ignored them. 'No laundry marks on his trousers, or boxers either. That's unusual these days. Someone at home does his laundry for him.' He jerked up the trousers, leaving them askew, then rolled the corpse on to its back again. He inspected the victim's hands and fingers. 'No defensive wounds. No calluses or scars. Should be able to get good prints once he dries out,' he said. 'He's dressed like a desk jockey and has soft hands, so he must push paper for a living. If he works for the government the FBI will have his fingerprints on file.' When he was finished examining the corpse Royal had to grab Tyson's arm to stand up. 'Left knee's messed up,' he said. 'Second Battle of the Marne. Never thought I'd see another war in my lifetime.'

Another black Chevy coupe with the District Metropolitan Police seal on its door pulled up and a policeman carrying a big Graflex camera got out.

'Get the victim full face and then all the other usual angles,' Royal said to him. 'And don't miss the lump behind his right ear.'

The photographer straddled the corpse and photographed the victim's face. He popped out a spent flashbulb, inserted a new one and took a second close-up. Then he rolled the corpse on its side to get a good shot of the victim's injury. He repositioned it, then proceeded to walk around the corpse, taking a few more shots from several different angles, then a few more of the shoreline of the Tidal Basin where the soldiers dragged the body up from the water. When he was done he picked up all his spent flashbulbs and tossed them in a nearby trashcan.

'OK,' Royal said, gesturing to the mortuary van drivers. 'Get this guy to the morgue pronto. Tell the doc to crack this guy's chest before he works on any natural deaths. We'll send over a fingerprint man tomorrow. And you,' he said to Tyson, 'get the soldier who discovered the body down to the precinct to give his statement right away.'

By now Tyson was about as star struck as an Army sergeant could be. He was a big fan of Erle Stanley Gardner and James M. Cain but he'd never met a real detective before.

'You think maybe he was murdered?' Tyson asked.

Royal shrugged. 'Don't know yet,' he said, 'but I intend to find out.'

Almost every seat at the long wooden tables in the OSS Reading Room was occupied. Files filled worktables, file carts and the return table. Some were stacked on the floor and a few empty chairs. Reference books, coffee cups, ashtrays and green-shaded reading lamps added to the disorder of the room. Tobacco smoke from dozens of cigarettes drifted upward and collected around the industrial lights dangling from the tall ceiling on long cords. A map of the world hung on one wall in a small area free of file cabinets. A frightening percentage of the world was outlined in black, indicating countries controlled by Germany and Japan.

The Reading Room operated much like a regular library. OSS staff and authorized visitors combed through the index card files and selected the files they wanted to read. They filled out slips of paper requesting those files. File girls took the slips and retrieved the files, listing the files and their readers in a bank-sized ledger. If the reader decided he or she wanted to remove files from the Reading Room and take them to their offices the file girls noted that in the ledger too. Later the ledgers themselves were filed away in case a document couldn't be found and needed to be traced. This happened fairly often, sending us on quests all over OSS. I once found a file of conversations between Archbishop Spellman and Pope Pius XII on the back of a toilet in a men's room in the Europe/ Africa division offices.

Girls in khaki work dresses or trousers swarmed the Registry and the Reading Room. Wearing cotton gloves to protect their hands and comfortable shoes they scurried about, picking up request slips, delivering files, then retrieving files from the return table to file them yet again. More girls pushing file carts roamed the OSS halls and offices to locate files that had been removed from the Reading Room that no one had bothered to return, or to find missing documents that someone was screaming for.

I recognized several OSS staff at one of the reading tables. I nodded at Spencer Benton from the Far Eastern Section but he didn't notice me. His wife worked at OSS too, as a typist. And I recognized the only woman at the tables but couldn't place her. Most of the OSS men wore uniforms since OSS had been militarized, but there were a few regular Army and Navy officers, as I could tell from their visitor badges and chest hardware. The few men in civilian clothes wearing visitor badges could be from the Department of State or even the White House.

A bored Army private stood watch over the door to the 'L' files reading room, where the documents from the Special Intelligence Section were kept. Those files couldn't be removed from the room. A person had to have special clearance to use them.

I found the stacks of ledgers and went through them until I found the one beginning with April 1, 1943. I hefted it into my arms and looked for an empty space at a table.

I squeezed into a chair between two men, one an Army colonel and the other a small elderly man with thick glasses in civilian clothes. Opening the ledger I skimmed it for Paul Hughes' name and signature.

The Army colonel shot me a suspicious glance.

'Compiling some statistics for Mr Lewis,' I said, responding to his unanswered question. The colonel shrugged and went back to his work, but I noticed he hid his own notes from me with his forearm.

I found Hughes' signature. The 'P' in Paul was florid, embellished with a wide loop, so I could easily identify it as I read down the narrow columns.

I skimmed the leaves of the ledger first, noting Hughes' signature regularly, then settled down to my task listing the files that he'd requested. My enthusiasm dimmed swiftly. Whatever the Security Office suspected Hughes of doing, the files he read seemed boring and innocuous to me. If he was a manpower expert, as Wicker had said, most of the files he read made perfect sense. They contained intelligence on German civilian labor, military losses gleaned from the obituary pages of German newspapers smuggled to Switzerland, estimates of Polish slave labor in Germany and OSS interviews with German exiles in Mexico.

But then I noted some inconsistencies. Why would Hughes be interested in the transportation network of the Soviet Union? Or estimates of the production of the Russian metallurgy industries? Or the location of the Red Army in the Mideast? This must be what Wicker wanted to know.

I needed a break. My eyes and throat stung from cigarette

smoke and dust and I needed to use the ladies' room. To protect my notes from prying eyes I took my notepad with me, stuffing it into my pocketbook, and closed the ledger, leaving behind in my seat a red 'reserved' card that meant I was coming back soon.

In the bathroom I cleaned my dust-coated glasses. Rooting around in my pocketbook I found some lozenges for my throat.

I wasn't alone long. The woman who had looked familiar to me entered the restroom but she didn't head for the toilets.

'I'm desperate to wash my hands,' she said. 'I swear the files I've got are covered with the sludge of centuries. Who knows where all the people who handle them have been?'

After washing up she stuck out her hand. 'I'm Rose Dudley,' she said, 'Spanish desk. I think we've met before.'

'I'm Louise Pearlie,' I said. 'I think we've met, too.'

'Probably at some office party,' she said. 'Where do you work?'

'I'm a file clerk in the Registry. Compiling statistics on file usage for my boss today.'

Rose opened her pocketbook and pulled out a packet of Luckies and a short ebony cigarette holder. She teased a cigarette out of the pack, squeezed it into the holder and held out the packet to me.

'No thanks,' I said.

'You must be the only person in this town who doesn't smoke,' Rose said, flicking her lighter into flame.

'I've tried,' I said. 'But it makes my throat sore.'

'Oh,' she said, immediately crushing her cigarette out in the bathroom sink.

'You don't have to do that,' I said. 'Really, I don't mind.'

'The last thing I need is another cigarette anyway,' she said, returning the packet and lighter to her purse. 'My voice is starting to sound like Jimmy Durante's.'

'If you're on the Spanish desk you must speak Spanish very well,' I said.

'Fluently.'

'Where did you go to college?' I asked.

She smiled at me widely. 'The Spanish Civil War,' she said.

'No kidding!' I was impressed.

'I was a stringer for a bunch of small Midwestern newspapers behind the lines,' she said. 'I only left my hotel in Madrid to go across the street to a restaurant for meals. Picked up everything I needed from Spanish radio and the men correspondents in the hotel bar. I wasn't getting paid enough to get shot at. And no, I've never met Ernest Hemingway! And you? What's your story?'

'I went to junior college and got married. When my husband died I worked for my parents. They own a fish camp on the coast of North Carolina. I sure prefer my job here to slinging fried bluefish and hush puppies.'

'If you're the Louise Pearlie I've heard about, you're quite the file clerk. Aren't you the girl who—?'

'I don't know what you're talking about,' I said, interrupting her. 'You shouldn't listen to gossip.'

We both giggled.

'I'm surprised you haven't been recruited into one of the operations divisions,' she said. 'If you were a man you would have been.'

She was right about that, but I didn't know her well enough to talk to her freely.

'I need to get back to work,' I said.

'Want to have lunch first?' she said.

'I'm going to work through lunch,' I said. 'I need to get this done by the end of the day.' I wanted to impress Wicker with my ability and I had a candy bar in my pocketbook to sustain me.

'Some other time then,' she said. 'I practically live in the Reading Room.'

'Sure.'

During the lunch hour the Reading Room was less crowded. The suspicious colonel had vacated the seat next to me so I had more elbow room. I munched on a Hershey's chocolate bar while I took more notes. Throughout the month Hughes' reading activity continued to focus on German labor and manpower.

But interspersed amongst the files describing fourteen-year-old boys working in German factories and the lowering of the German military draft age were some totally unrelated subjects. Like the organization and policies of the British intelligence services. And material compiled by our Foreign Nationalities Branch on racial groups in the United States. What did that have to do with German manpower?

I found myself making excuses for Hughes. The files were open to any staff from OSS. Who knew why he was straying from his own field? His boss might have asked him to look something up for him. His reading of these files was meaningless without some other suspicious information about him. Which, I assumed, OSS Security must have.

It was a waste of time for me to be curious. I would probably never know why I'd been asked to do this job.

When I finally finished and looked up from my task my eyes were so tired I couldn't focus on the wall clock. I took off my glasses, rubbed my eyes and slipped my specs back on. It was five thirty. I'd finished the job in a day.

After folding my notes into a letter-sized brown envelope I carried it over to OSS headquarters and up to Mr Lewis's office. His door was closed and I asked his secretary to let him know I was here, that I had information for him.

She reached for the envelope. 'I'll give it to him,' she said.

'I'm sorry,' I said, 'I'm supposed to hand it to him personally.'

'That's absurd.'

'Those are my instructions.'

'I can't interrupt Mr Lewis,' she said. 'I assure you I'll see that he has your letter the next time he calls me into his office.'

'I'm not giving this document to you and I'm not leaving,' I said. Then I added, 'It's Top Secret.'

She looked me over. I was a lowly file clerk wearing a military-blue tailored dress that sold by the hundreds at J.C. Penney. She was secretary to a division head and I suspected her suit was a Fred Block. It had his signature leather cuffs.

'You can't have that kind of clearance!' she said.

'But I do.'

She gave in but she wasn't happy about it. When she lifted up the phone and spoke to Lewis on the intercom her voice sounded a tone higher. She slammed the receiver down.

'All right,' she said, 'you can go in.'

Lewis looked up from his desk.

'Finished?' he asked.

'Yes, I . . .'

'Don't say anything,' he said, checking to make sure that I had signed the envelope across the back flap. 'I'll take care of it. You may go.'

I didn't move and he looked at me impatiently.

'I'm supposed to watch you lock it in your safe,' I said.

'Oh, right, of course.'

I officially observed Lewis as he placed the document in his safe and twirled the knob. Then I left. I suspected that would be the last I ever saw of Mr Wilmarth Lewis. I wondered if I'd hear from Major Wicker and OSS Security again. I was curious about Hughes. I wanted to know what OSS suspected he had done.

After the record-breaking cold of the winter of 1943, walking home in springtime was a treat. Most District residents had converted their gardens into vegetable plots but there were still nooks filled with daffodils and lilies. An occasional rose-bush climbed over a picket fence and blooming redbud trees filled the pink gap emptied by the end of cherry blossom season. Being outdoors was a respite from the hours I spent bent over a desk, and I loved the exercise.

My boarding house was on 'I' Street, south of the fashion-able addresses that began on 'K', and continued north to Dupont Circle. My landlady, Phoebe Holcombe, had been wealthy before the Depression. After the death of her husband she somehow still had a little money. She'd opened the doors of her home to boarders for patriotic reasons and to take her mind off her two sons who served in the Pacific. I'd been lucky to find a room here. 'Two Trees' was much less crowded than most boarding houses in Washington. I even had my own room and shared a bathroom with just two other women, Phoebe and another boarder, Ada Herman. Ada hailed from New York City. Formerly a music teacher, now she played clarinet in the Willard Hotel and made pots of money doing it. Ada and I had a special bond. One night she confessed to me that she had married a German Lufthansa airline pilot before the war. He'd left her to return to Nazi Germany to join the Luftwaffe. She didn't dare begin divorce proceedings. If anyone knew she was married to a Nazi she might well be interned. Her late nights partying, all her beaus, the dyed platinum blonde hair and wardrobe full of divine clothes disguised the terror she lived with every day. I know she prayed for her husband's death, I heard her at night through the wall between our bedrooms. After that first conversation we had never spoken of her husband again. She trusted me to keep her secret and I would. I kept plenty more. I was beginning to think of myself as the Fort Knox of secrets!

The front door was unlocked at this time of day so I went straight into the small entry hall and hung my straw fedora on the hat stand. I pulled off my cotton gloves and tossed them and my pocketbook on to the small chair in the hall next to the table that held our telephone. The mail rested on the hall table. I flipped through the envelopes. There was nothing for me and I felt my eyes begin to sting. But I shook off my disappointment and forced the tears back. Joe couldn't write every day, he was busy, he was doing important work. That was why he'd been transferred to the New York office of the Joint Distribution Committee, the Jewish organization dedicated to rescuing and finding refuge for Jewish refugees. Of course no one besides me in this house knew that was his job. Teaching Slavic languages at George Washington University had been his cover story. I'd found out his real work by accident. Supposedly Joe was in New York City to teach a class of second-generation Slavs to speak their native languages so fluently they could translate once the Allies invaded their countries. Another secret!

Following the tantalizing odor of dinner cooking I made my way back to the kitchen, Dellaphine's domain. Sure enough she was standing at the stove barefoot, stirring a pot of simmering chicken parts, her milk chocolate face damp from the steam.

'Welcome home, Miss Louise,' she said. 'How was work?'

'Same as always,' I said. 'You?'

'Me too.'

She drew a letter from her apron pocket and handed it to me. 'Here's a letter for you, from Mr Joe, I sneaked it just as soon as the mailman came. I figured you wouldn't want Mr Henry or Miss Ada to see it so soon after you got the last one.'

I wrapped my arms around her skinny body and hugged her hard.

'You're an angel and a pearl above price,' I said to her.

'Get away, silly girl, I got work to do and you are in my way.' She gave me a friendly push and went into her pantry looking for flour for her dumplings.

I headed outside, but not before pulling off my socks and saddle shoes so I could walk barefoot in the grass. I slipped down the back stairs and under the dark staircase before I ripped open the letter.

Joe, who was Czech, though he had a British passport, wrote English rather formally.

He began 'My Dear Louise', and finished with 'Most Sincerely Yours'. It wasn't a love letter at first. He wrote as though to a friend, newsy paragraphs about meeting new people and exploring New York City. From his borrowed flat he could see the Williamsburg Bridge over the East River and walk to Broadway. But his last sentence was personal. 'Louise, my love, please save me from my misery and tell me that you are coming to visit me soon.'

Joe and I had come very close to becoming lovers while he lived here. But we were afraid Phoebe would discover us and be so shocked she'd send me away and I couldn't afford an apartment on my own. Washington was just too crowded. And I was worried about my job.

Having an affair with a foreign refugee was not a good way for an OSS employee to keep her Top Secret clearance and her job.

So Joe's transfer was at first a relief to both of us. But when we discovered that an old friend could lend Joe his flat in Williamsburg we realized that I could travel to New York for weekends and could enjoy our affair in anonymity. Of course I had agreed. I just didn't know when I could go. I felt a hot flush spread from my groin upward until my face burned. Misery, indeed!

I shoved the letter into my pocket just in time.

'Louise,' Ada said. 'What on earth are you doing standing under the staircase? And in your bare feet! It's so damp. You'll catch a cold.' Ada had just come home from playing clarinet for a tea dance at the Willard. She was still wearing a silk dress and heels.

'Don't be silly, city girl!' I said, wiggling my toes in the cool earth. 'It feels good! And I am going into the basement to check on the baby chicks.'

'You can get into the basement from the kitchen.'

'I went to look at the garden first.'

Henry, our male boarder, and I had dug up every last bit of the back yard that got enough sun to grow vegetables. We'd already eaten spring greens from it – early lettuce and spinach – and the tomatoes, corn, squash and potatoes were coming along nicely.

'Come see the chicks with me, they're so sweet,' I said to Ada.

The previous winter had been too severe for last year's flock of chickens to survive outside in their coop. We'd had no choice but to sacrifice them to Dellaphine's cast-iron skillet. This spring Phoebe and I had bought twenty baby Plymouth Rock chicks to replace them. I loved the adult Plymouth Rocks' black and white stripes. Right now they were just soft fuzzy black babies.

As soon as Ada and I went into the basement I heard the chicks peeping. We were raising them in a cage near the boiler until they were large enough to go outside into the chicken coop. They had plenty of food and water. Henry had rigged up a light bulb to keep them warm.

'God, do they ever stop peeping?' Ada asked.

'Not until they're grown,' I said. I scooped a tiny bit of chirping fluff up into my hand. Its peeping ratcheted up a couple of notches. 'Just touch her,' I said. Ada reached out a hand and patted the chick's head. 'She's so soft and tiny,' she said. 'I think we got a healthy batch,' I said, placing the frantic chick back in the cage with her sisters. 'We've only lost one. And there's just one rooster.' We'd requested all hens but it was difficult to sex baby chicks and the seller couldn't guarantee every chick was a female. We'd have the rooster for Sunday dinner once he began to crow and annoy the neighbors.

The pathologist lit a cigarette after he pulled a sheet over the victim's head.

'So, doc, what's the scoop?' Detective Royal said. 'Did he drown, or what?'

'Oh, he drowned all right,' the pathologist said. 'His lungs and airway are full of water. But I can't say for sure it was an accident.'

Royal stubbed out his own cigarette on the steel examining table before pulling a narrow notebook and pencil from his topcoat pocket.

'Why do you say that?' he asked.

'Well,' the pathologist answered. 'It's the lump on the back of his head that concerns me. His skull was fractured. Now he could have fallen and hit his head on a rock and rolled into the water. The shoreline of the Tidal Basin is sloped and lined with rocks. Or he could have been blotto, there's some alcohol in his bloodstream. But it could also be that he was intention-ally hit on the head and thrown into the water.'

'You can't tell if he got the head injury before or after he went into the water?'

The pathologist shook his head. 'That's not within my power. Sorry.' He flicked off the bright examining light and flung the stark morgue into dimness. The only natural light in the room came from a tall glass window with a red stained-glass cross embedded in it. The red shaft of light lit up the long room of refrigerated metal drawers that lined the morgue wall opposite the window.

Royal stopped taking notes. 'Seems to me that this can't be an accident since his pockets were empty. Where was his wallet?'

'That's your area of expertise, not mine,' the pathologist said. 'Your fingerprint guy was here earlier by the way, he said he got good prints.'

'Yeah,' Royal said, 'we sent them off to the FBI. Their fingerprint girls are the best. If his are on file we should know within a week.'

Royal was an old-fashioned detective, trained long before the FBI had begun to analyze blood and hair and laundry marks. He knew that once the victim was identified all he had to do was retrace the victim's previous twenty-four hours to find out what had happened to him. It wasn't always easy, but it worked.

'Churchill arrived today,' Henry said, helping himself to a steaming bowl of Dellaphine's chicken and dumplings. 'I read he's staying at the White House, not at the British Embassy with the rest of the delegation.'

'I'm surprised by that,' Phoebe said. 'Eleanor Roosevelt cannot stand the man. He drinks all day, and those awful cigars!'

Churchill and an assortment of British lords, admirals and generals, including Lord Louis Mountbatten, had just arrived in Washington for the Trident Conference to plan an invasion of Europe. In April the American and British navies had driven the Nazi submarine fleet back to its den at Saint-Nazaire for good, clearing the Atlantic for allied transport and supply ships. It was time to make plans to conquer Italy, bomb Germany into dust and take Europe back from the Nazis. That was one reason the Reading Room was jammed with OSS staff. They were answering queries coming in by the hour from the American delegates to the Trident Conference.

Every single power involved in this war desperately wanted to know what the Americans and British were discussing at Trident, even their allies. Obviously the conference was the target of dozens of spies. Which might be why OSS Security was so interested in the files Paul Hughes had been reading.

'The *Washington Post* seems quite optimistic about the course of the war,' Ada said. 'One of the editorials predicted we'd invade soon.'

Not for a year at least, I thought. If then. The effort required would be unprecedented.

'Things are looking up,' Henry said. 'I just hope Roosevelt listens to Churchill.'

Looking up only in the sense that planning for the real war could begin. Yes, Rommel had been defeated in North Africa, the North Atlantic shipping lanes were clear, but Germany had an iron grip on Europe. What did they call it? Fortress Europe?

'I heard,' said Ada, who'd changed into a black dress for her gig that night, 'that Churchill sleeps until noon and has a scotch and water even before he gets out of bed! And that he wanders around his rooms naked after his bath!'

I'd been told the same story at work. Apparently President Roosevelt surprised the Prime Minister after his bath, rolling quietly into Churchill's bedroom in the middle of the afternoon. 'Well, Mr President,' Churchill had said, 'at least there's nothing coming between us.'

Phoebe tapped her glass with her spoon and cleared her throat.

'I'd like to tell you all something I've been keeping quiet about for a long time.' she said, 'because I'm so excited about it I didn't want to jinx it.'

'Hurry up and tell us, then,' Henry said.

'Yes, Phoebe, please do!' Ada said.

What was this, I wondered?

Still Phoebe hesitated, as if she couldn't quite bring herself to say such wonderful words.

'I told you that Milt Junior was injured at Guadalcanal,' she said. 'Not seriously. He's been in a hospital in Adelaide.

Well, he's coming home! For two weeks leave!' Phoebe twisted her napkin into a ball and beamed.

'Oh, Phoebe, I'm so happy for you,' I said. 'That's grand!'

'How thrilling,' Ada said. 'You must be so excited!'

Henry nodded, agreeing. 'I'm looking forward to meeting the boy,' he said. 'When does he arrive?'

'I don't really know yet,' Phoebe said. 'I'll get a telegram in the next few days.'

Dellaphine brought a tray into the room and began to load up our dirty dishes.

'Did you know about Milt?' Ada asked her.

'Yes ma'am,' Dellaphine said. 'It's mighty good news.'

We could all only guess at the worry Phoebe had experienced since her sons had been in the Pacific. She'd lost weight in the year and a half I'd been living here. And it seemed she took more and more Nembutal as the weeks went by. Sherry evenings were more frequent too. Dellaphine was concerned, I could tell by the way she looked when the Peoples Drug Store van delivered Ada's prescription. Phoebe must be so relieved. Tom, her younger son, was safeguarding military supplies on some remote Pacific island behind the lines. And now Milt was coming home on leave.

Dellaphine brought in the dessert, green grapes suspended in red cherry Jell-O. I ate it because I was hungry, but Jell-O was on my list of foods never to eat after the war ended, ever!

After Phoebe and Henry went into the lounge Ada caught me up in the hall. She took me by the arm.

'My taxi's waiting, I have to get to work,' she said. 'I hate to sound selfish, but where is Milt going to sleep?' The same question had crossed my mind. Surely Phoebe wouldn't want Milt to sleep up in the attic bedroom with Henry. That left our rooms.

'It's just for a couple of weeks,' I said. 'We could take turns sleeping on the sofa.'

'I have a friend I might be able to crash with for a while,' Ada said. 'I would hate to lose my room here.'

'Me, too,' I said.

'Do you think we could share an apartment?' she said. 'Our

different hours might drive us both loony, though.' If Ada and I shared a two-and-a-half, which would be all I could afford, it would have one living room, one bedroom and a kitchenette. We'd have to share the bedroom. Ada could afford an apartment of her own, but the District Housing Authority wouldn't be likely to approve it.

'Let's just hope it works out so we can stay here,' Ada said. 'It's hard to imagine living somewhere else now.'

Ada went out the front door to her waiting taxi and I went into the lounge to join Phoebe and Henry. The sherry service was on the table and Henry and Phoebe were already raising glasses to toast Milt's homecoming. I was happy to join them.

When I got to work the next morning Pat, the messenger, was sitting on the corner of my desk waiting for me.

'Mrs Pearlie,' he said, 'Don't put down your things. You're wanted in Mr Lewis's office right away.'

I glanced over at Jesse Shera, my boss, who stood nearby. He nodded his OK to me.

Once more I walked across the street into the main OSS compound and up the wide stairs of the former naval hospital to the top floor hall where the OSS big shots had their offices. Lewis's secretary barely acknowledged me as she waved me into his office.

Lewis wasn't there. Instead Major Angus Wicker waited for me in one of the leather chairs. His uniform was even more wrinkled than it had been yesterday.

'Good morning, Mrs Pearlie,' he said. 'Please sit down.'

I sat, feeling oddly uncomfortable with my hat and pocketbook in my lap.

'I need your assistance again today,' he said.

Oh goody. Making lists of files was only slightly more interesting than cataloguing and filing and would lose its appeal to me very soon.

'Mr Hughes isn't at work again today,' he said. 'And he hasn't called us.'

'What do you think has happened?' I asked.

'We have no idea,' Wicker said, 'and it concerns us.'

He uncrossed his legs and leaned toward me.

'You saw yesterday that some of the files he checked out of the Reading Room were, shall we say, not in Mr Hughes' area of study. We don't suspect him of anything yet, not at all. But with the Trident Conference in town, let's just say that allied intelligence is a valuable commodity.'

I could feel the pulse beating in my temple. Was Hughes passing OSS intelligence? If so, to whom? Ally or enemy?

'I need a jolly girl such as yourself to drop by Mr Hughes' boarding house,' he said. 'Talk to his landlady. Just say he's been missed at work and there's concern about his whereabouts. You can pretend to be a secretary sent by his boss. You won't need to say what office you're from, no one expects that these days.'

'There's no telephone at his boarding house?'

'The landlady doesn't have one.' That wasn't unusual. It took months to get permission from the War Production Board to buy a telephone.

'All right, of course,' I said. 'Right now?'

'Right now. As if you'd gotten to work and your boss sent you out right away. Here's the address.' Wicker handed me an index card. It read '905 25th Street'; that was in Foggy Bottom, a neighborhood north of OSS headquarters and west of my own. I tucked the card in my pocketbook.

'And this,' he said, handing me another slip of paper, 'is my direct telephone number. If I don't answer it, my secretary will. Memorize it.'

I did, and gave the paper back to him.

'And,' he said, giving me an envelope and a form, 'some cash for the bus and lunch. Please sign the receipt.' I did so and began to feel my heart rate surge. An adventure loomed!

Maybe few people would think that taking the bus to a boarding house and asking a landlady the whereabouts of a boarder was exciting, but I did! As the bus wound its way through the streets of Foggy Bottom I found myself picturing wild scenarios about Hughes for which I had no evidence whatsoever.

Hughes could be a German mole, planted in the United States years ago, who'd mined the OSS files for intelligence, slipped it to the Nazis, and now had fled. Maybe to Mexico. I had previous experience with an embedded Nazi spy, so I knew it wasn't impossible. Or perhaps Hughes had gone underground, with a new cover story, and was hidden in a closet at the Federal Reserve Building where the Trident Conference was being held, tuned in to several listening devices, ready to sell his information to the highest bidder. No one could say I didn't have a vivid imagination.

I got off the bus at 25th Street and went down the street, stopping in front of a tiny cottage, part of a short row of similar cottages that I suspected were once servants' quarters for the double row house on the corner. I double-checked the address. This place was way too small for a boarding house. But I had the right place so I walked up to the front door and knocked. I could hear a radio playing classical music inside.

I was just about to knock again when the front door opened revealing a little elderly woman wearing a pink apron studded with embroidered strawberries. She used way too much bluing in her hair.

'Yes,' she said, 'can I help you?'

'Mrs Nighy?' I asked.

'Yes.'

'My name is Louise Pearlie,' I began.

'Do come in,' she said, 'the sun is making my eyes water.'

Entering a dark hallway I glimpsed a lounge off to the left where Mrs Nighy had set up her ironing board. Two cats, one black and one a tabby, regarded me lazily from a davenport. The house was so small I could see all four rooms from where I stood. A half-closed door at the back of the house, opposite the kitchen, showed a slice of what had to be Mrs Nighy's bedroom. Lots of pink flounced across the window curtains and a knitting project lay across the bed. In front of the house, across from the lounge (this door ajar too), I saw Hughes' room. The embroidered white curtains at the window were feminine, but the trousers thrown across the foot of the bed belonged to a man.

I heard a kitchen timer sound off.

'Oh dear,' Mrs Nighy said, 'let me get my biscuits out of the oven and I'll be right back.'

When she turned toward the kitchen I slipped into Hughes' room. I hoped Mrs Nighy moved slowly.

Hughes' dopp kit sat on his dresser. His desk held a map of Europe secured by a glass with a quarter inch of brown liquid in it. It smelled like bourbon. A battered leather briefcase, a narrow one secured with a flap that buckled, rested on the desk chair. Holding my breath I flipped open the satchel flap. There were no OSS files or documents inside. In fact there was nothing in the satchel except a half-sheet of notepaper that read 'G. Sunday 9th'. Quickly I stuffed the note in my pocket.

I was waiting, a little breathless, for Mrs Nighy when she came back into the hall.

'Do come sit down,' she said, leading me into the lounge.

I sat in a faded pink wing chair, one of a pair on either side of a petite fireplace meant to burn coal, and she took the other.

The black cat jumped off the davenport and meandered over to us, lying down on the rug between us as if to protect her owner.

'I'm doing my ironing,' Mrs Nighy said. 'I just have the one boarder, and the laundries are so busy, it's no bother to wash and iron his things.'

'Speaking about your boarder,' Louise said, 'I'm calling to ask you about him. Paul Hughes?'

'Yes,' she said. 'Such a lovely man. No trouble at all. I was lucky to draw his name. He's quite tidy and so quiet. He reads in his room every evening after dinner. Rarely goes out except to visit his mother on the weekends.'

'As I was saying,' I said, 'I'm from his office. He hasn't been to work for two days, and we haven't heard from him. You don't have a telephone, I suppose?'

She glanced at a drum table, where a telephone must once have stood.

'No,' she said, 'my old one couldn't be repaired and I haven't been able to get it replaced.'

'Is Mr Hughes in town? Have you heard from him?'

'No,' she said, 'he's not here. He left to visit his mother in Fredericksburg and hasn't returned.'

My heart skipped a beat. Was Hughes on the lam?

'But I've had a telegram from his mother,' Mrs Nighy said. 'Just a minute.' She went into her tiny kitchen and came back with a square of paper. 'He's ill,' she said, 'and can't come home until he's better.'

She handed me a Western Union telegram dated last Sunday evening.

'My son Paul is ill stop cannot travel stop more later stop,' the telegram said. It was signed 'Mrs Hughes'. That was all. There was no return address on the telegram, which wasn't unusual. The Western Union code of numbers and letters above the message could tell us from which office the telegram was sent. Out of habit I memorized it.

'This has concerned me so,' Mrs Nighy said. 'I haven't heard anything since. I don't know his mother's phone number or address. And of course I couldn't call Mr Hughes' office since I don't know where he works.'

I didn't enlighten her.

'Can I take this back to my office?' I asked. 'Perhaps we can find a way to contact Mrs Hughes.'

'Would you let me know what you learn, please?'

'Of course,' I said.

I went back to OSS with two scraps of information. A Western Union telegram and a cryptic note on half a sheet of notepaper. On the bus I reviewed what had happened so far. On Tuesday, May 11, Hughes didn't show up for work and I was asked to take notes on his file usage. On Wednesday he still wasn't at work. I was sent to his lodgings, where his landlady handed over to me a telegram from Hughes' mother indicating that

Hughes was ill. It had been sent Sunday the 9th. In Hughes'
room I'd found a note referring to a meeting with 'G' on that
same Sunday. The circumstances of Hughes' disappearance
were suspicious, all right. OSS Security would track him like
a coon until he was found, even if that turned out to be in an
innocent sickbed at his mother's and 'G' was his barber!

I wanted desperately to be involved in the search for Hughes.
Going back to the file room, never to hear the answers to all
these questions, would drive me to the loony bin!

TWO

When you have to use older women, try to get ones who have worked outside the home at some time in their lives. [. . .] older women who have never contacted the public have a hard time adapting themselves, and are inclined to be cantankerous and fussy. It's always well to impress on older women the importance of friendliness and courtesy.

'1943 Guide to Hiring Women', *Mass Transportation*
magazine, July 1943.

I turned over the telegram and the note I found in Hughes' room to Wicker.

'Well,' was all he said, as he sat studying the telegram and the note. Then after a minute he said 'Huh'. I shuffled in my seat. He looked up at me and nodded dismissively. 'Thank you for all your help, Mrs Pearlie,' he said. 'Good work.'

I hesitated to rise from the chair. 'Major Wicker,' I said, 'I can trace the telegram from the Western Union code. Hughes' next of kin will be listed in his personnel file. Once we have Mrs Hughes' address we can find her telephone number. If she doesn't have a telephone perhaps we could reach her through a neighbor. We have research materials in the Registry that I can access quickly.'

Wicker seemed not to have noticed I was still in his office. He glanced over at me. 'What?' he said. I repeated myself. 'Oh, yes, Mrs Pearlie, of course. But we'll take it from here on out.' He smiled at me. 'We have resources too.'

I left Smith's office and Wicker. The secretary didn't bother to notice me as she typed away from her shorthand notebook.

I was furious. Damn Wicker! One minute he tells me

how important this task is, the next he treats me like an eighteen-year-old!

As I stamped down three flights of steps and across the street to my own office I forced myself to calm down. OSS was an intelligence agency. It was neatly sectioned so that no one knew more than he or she needed to, except for the top men. Raiding another section for help with the clerical work of examining Hughes' file usage, and even calling on Mrs Nighy, had been a clever thing for Wicker to do. He knew from my personnel file that I could be counted on to keep my mouth shut. Perhaps he had good reason to let few people at OSS know that Hughes' absence might be questionable. Anyway, no matter how curious I was, it was out of my hands. Who knew, Wicker could well be on a wild goose chase. I might see Hughes wandering around OSS tomorrow, fully recovered from the flu! And with an acceptable reason for checking out files that weren't in his field. Though I was sure I would go to my grave wondering who the hell 'G' was!

As I crossed 'E' Street for the second time that day I skirted a pothole brimming with spring rainfall. The air was clean and fresh from another brisk morning shower. This would be another day I wouldn't need to water our garden. I resolved to forget all about Paul Hughes and spend my evening reading *Hungry Hill*. It was overdue at the library.

So I resolutely filed away all my questions about Hughes and focused on summarizing and indexing the usual stacks of intelligence documents. All of them were boring numbers and statistics, except for one about Hitler's contingency plan to escape to Japan by air if Germany fell. It had been told to an OSS operative in a bar in Switzerland by a very drunk 'reliable source'. The 'documents' were paper napkins stained with wine glass rings. Red wine.

I filled my tray at the OSS cafeteria with tuna casserole, cabbage salad and canned pineapple. It was edible, but I looked forward to the fresh vegetables from our Victory Garden.

I squeezed in at a table next to Joan Adams and Betty Burnette. Joan was my closest friend in Washington. She worked for General Donovan himself. Not surprising, since she was older than most government girls, from a wealthy California oil family, and had gone to Smith College. She fit in well with Donovan's crowd.

She was also an old maid, and hated it.

We had to lean our heads together and shout over the din of clattering trays and conversations to hear each other. Although we had gotten pretty good at reading each other's lips!

'How's the Scotsman?' I asked her.

'Gone back to Britain,' she said.

'Oh, I'm sorry,' I said.

'Orders. He said he'd write, but I know how that goes.'

'He'll write,' Betty said, 'He really likes you.' Betty spoke from the optimistic vantage point of a young, pretty, blonde newly-wed. She had been a gently used government girl with mediocre prospects until she fell in love with a middle-aged District policeman named Ralph Burnette. He adored Betty despite an unfortunate misjudgment that landed her in jail for a few days. In fact, they had met there. I didn't understand it but they seemed quite happy.

'We did have a lot of fun together,' Joan said, 'but I'll wait until I see an airgraph with a Scottish postmark in my mailbox before I'll hope to see him again.'

A familiar-looking woman set her tray on the corner of our table. 'Do you mind if I sit here?' she asked, grabbing a chair from another table seconds after it was vacated.

Betty and I scrunched further together so that there'd be room for her.

'Thanks,' the woman said. 'My name is Peggy Benton.' Spencer Benton's wife, I thought.

'Peggy works with me in the typing pool,' Betty said. 'Three desks to the south.'

'I've met your husband,' I said. 'I work in the Registry. I see him in the Reading Room almost every day.'

'He's ruining his eyes and his health,' she said, tucking her napkin in her lap. 'But he won't listen to me.'

'Do you have any children?' Joan asked, her thoughts as always on the domestic state.

'No,' Peggy said. 'Not with the war on. Maybe after.'

'We were discussing boyfriends,' Betty said.

'No we weren't,' Joan said.

'Louise dates a university professor,' Betty said to Peggy. I saw a frown cross Joan's face. She deeply disapproved of Joe. She didn't think I should even be friendly with a refugee with a Slavic accent.

'Not any more I don't,' I said.

'Really?' Joan asked. She tucked into a slice of honey cake. She was a large woman who loved to eat.

'Joe moved to New York City,' I said. 'He's teaching at NYU now. They're short on Slavic language professors there.'

'Where does this Joe come from?' Peggy asked.

'He's Czech,' I said, 'but he's lived in England most of his life. He's got a British passport.'

'Is he a Communist then?' Peggy asked, picking diced pickles out of her macaroni and cheese.

'Good God,' Joan said, 'what a question!'

'Why?' Peggy asked. 'All the Eastern Europeans here are Communists. Or socialists. Except for the royalty, of course.'

I didn't feel comfortable answering her question. I barely knew Peggy Benton. And I didn't want to put words in Joe's mouth.

'Joe wants the Allies to win the war,' I said. 'Just like the rest of us. That's all he's ever expressed to me.'

Peggy shrugged.

'Peggy is really interested in politics and the news,' Betty said. 'She's always reading the newspaper on her break. I can't wait to win the war either. Then Ralph and I can buy a house with our war bonds.'

Despite my earlier resolution my curiosity about Paul Hughes refused to go away. I had ten minutes yet before I was due back at my desk. It seemed to me that if Paul Hughes hadn't been seen since the weekend except for a telegram from his mother – and today was Wednesday – that was most peculiar. I supposed he could be delirious with flu somewhere. Did he ever get to meet 'G' on Sunday? Was meeting 'G' part of his work, or an independent rendezvous? Who could I pump for information about him?

I stopped on the sidewalk outside the huge apartment house on 'E' Street, across from the main OSS campus, that was the headquarters of the Research and Analysis Division of OSS.

The Registry, the library really, was a vital division of R&A, which had six hundred scholar/spies working on evaluating and analyzing overt and covert intelligence. Several of these scholar/spies owed me a favor.

It was my lucky day. Don Murray walked out of the front door with his pipe in his hand. He sat down on the steps, stretched out his legs and pulled his tobacco pouch out of his jacket pocket. I knew Don well. Before the OSS reorganization he'd been my boss. I'd solved an embarrassing problem for him. We'd even dated a few times until he realized I wouldn't be as appropriate a wife as he'd thought, which saved me the trouble of jilting him. Now he was head of the economic subdivision of the Europe/Africa division. He'd know Paul Hughes.

I patted my hair and adjusted my skirt before going over to him.

'Hi,' I said.

Don stopped drawing on his pipe. He seemed pleased to see me.

'Louise!' he said. 'Do you have time to chat?'

'Sure,' I said, gathering my legs sedately under me and sitting down one step below him. I noted that we were far enough down the stairs for the GI guarding the door not to hear us.

'How are you?' he asked. 'Are you liking your new job?'

'At times,' I said. 'And yours?'

'It's not much different from what I did before, although

it's more oriented toward military strategy than it used to be. But you know that.'

He drew on his pipe. He smoked a different tobacco than Joe. I longed for its odor.

'I need a favor, Don,' I said.

'Sure. If I can do it I will,' he said.

I lowered my voice. 'Has anyone heard from Paul Hughes? Do you know where he is?'

Don groaned. 'The rumors have started already! Why do you want to know?'

'Just curious. Is it a secret?'

'No,' he said, 'the entire Division knows he hasn't been heard from since he left work on Friday. I did hear a rumor that he might be ill, but that's all I can say. Don't spread it around, OK?'

'You know me better than that,' I said.

Something about missing the odor of Joe's pipe tobacco plunged me into a despondency deeper than I had felt since arriving in Washington. Ever since Joe had left for his new job in New York life seemed so tedious.

Even parts of my life that had no relation to Joe were less appealing to me now that he wasn't around. The importance of my work, my financial freedom and my new friends, none of them filled that hole in my life that he'd left. Or were as much fun as they had been.

I pulled a file from my in-box on to my desk. It contained several single-spaced, typed sheets on onionskin paper, with multiple cross-outs and typos and an occasional foray into French. Far from being intrigued by it I just wanted to stick it on the bottom of the pile and do something challenging that would take my mind off my problems – like find out where Paul Hughes was!

Instead I focused on the intelligence in front of me. Its puzzle drove Joe out of my mind. The document came in a diplomatic pouch from Lisbon with no provenance attached. According to our agent's memo it had been slipped into the covert mail slot he kept at a tobacconist's by person or persons unknown. Clearly the thin sheets were the carbon copies of another document. The blue carbon ink bled into the crevices of the thin cheap paper. I opened my top drawer and drew out a magnifying glass and set about deciphering the papers. Before long I was engrossed in the subject matter. It appeared to be a carbon copy of a poorly typed document concerning British diplomatic attempts to sign a separate peace treaty with Hitler. It was crinkled up as if it had been tossed in a trashcan. I had no way of knowing if this was a real document or Nazi disinformation designed to divide the Allies. Once I finished the index cards I didn't file them. I walked the cards and the document over to the X-2 Branch. An expert there would decide if the material was genuine.

It wasn't until I stepped outside the door to walk home that despondency settled on me once more. I felt that I had nothing to look forward to. Joe and I had planned a summer of fun. Concerts at the Watergate, barbecues on Rock Creek, exploring the Virginia side of the Potomac by canoe, seeing all the new movies. And yes, spending as many weekends as we could on his friend's houseboat on the Potomac. Alone.

But our romantic plans fell apart. Because of me. I'd backed out. I was afraid that an affair with Joe would jeopardize my place in Phoebe's house, and maybe even my job. I couldn't afford an apartment on my own. And OSS frowned on women with Top Secret clearance having love affairs with foreign refugees. And besides, how did I know that anything Joe said about his background and his work was the truth? I'd already learned that his 'professorship' was a cover. I loved him, but he was still keeping secrets from me.

I felt tears form and slipped behind the building so no one in the crowds of government workers collecting at the bus stop at the main entrance of the building would see my distress. Once I had backed out of the relationship with Joe, living together in the same house became torture because we were still so attracted to each other. And then Joe was reassigned to New York with a new cover. Or at least that's what he told me. And then a new, enticing possibility opened. I could visit Joe there on the occasional weekend, away from the prying eyes of my friends, my landlady and my OSS colleagues, and we could have our wartime love affair. With no strings attached. An arrangement that would never have crossed my mind a year ago. But then I wasn't the woman who'd left Wilmington, North Carolina, in January 1942. Not anymore.

The truth was I still hadn't made up my mind.

'Are you all right?' Rose Dudley asked. She put a hand on my shoulder. 'I don't mean to intrude,' she said. 'Aren't you feeling well?'

'I'm OK,' I said, wiping lingering tears from my eyelashes.

'It's a wonder we aren't sobbing all the time, the way the world is,' she said, linking her arm in mine.

I smiled at that. So true. How silly to pine over a lover when the world was in flames.

'Listen,' Rose said, 'my room-mate and I like to have friends over on Thursday evenings, girls like us who like to work and have the same opinions. You are a New Dealer, aren't you?'

'Yes, of course,' I said.

'We don't talk about anything we shouldn't, just the news and some harmless gossip, and we don't have to worry about what we say. We have cocktails, snacks, and play records. Sometimes we invite a man friend or two, but they have to be well behaved.'

'Sounds lovely,' I said. Since Joe left there wasn't anyone at my boarding house I could really talk to. I was fond of Ada and Phoebe but I had little in common with them. Joan was a swell friend but her crowd had all gone to college and had family money. Sometimes I felt uncomfortable around them.

Rose squeezed my arm. 'So you'll come?'

'Yes, I'd love to.' Finally, something to look forward to!

'Here,' Rose said, digging around in her purse and pulling out a little pad in a leather case with a tiny pen attached. She scribbled something, tore it off the pad and gave it to me. 'Here's the address, see you Thursday!' Rose lived in the Potomac House Apartments, a big complex in Foggy Bottom. I could walk there in good weather.

Like much of the District, Foggy Bottom had become more like a barracks for government workers than a true neighborhood. It was studded with apartment complexes and nearly every row house or cottage took in boarders. Mrs Nighy's little cottage, where Paul Hughes boarded, was just across the street from Rose's apartment building.

'Thank you,' I said, tucking the address into my own pocketbook. 'What time?'

'Seven,' she said. 'We break up around nine thirty. We working girls need our sleep, you know. Lord, there's my bus!' Rose dropped my arm and took off running, waving her hat to keep the bus driver from leaving her behind.

Henry was waiting for me by the gate.

'What's wrong?' I asked him.

He took my arm. 'It's Phoebe,' he said. 'I wanted to warn you before you came inside.'

'Is she ill?'

'No,' he said, glancing back at the house. 'But her nerves are real bad. Milt was more gravely wounded than he told his mother. He's OK. He called Phoebe from Walter Reed this afternoon. He's been there for a week already and this is the first time she knew he was even back in the country.'

I found Phoebe inside the lounge. She sagged on the davenport, with her head propped against a cushion and a hand shielding her eyes. Ada sat close to her holding her free hand.

'Phoebe,' I said. 'I just heard about Milt. I'm so sorry! He is going to be all right, though, isn't he?'

Phoebe turned to me. Her eyes were dilated. Nembutal. I didn't pass judgment. I'd popped a few of her pills myself.

'He's going to be just fine,' she said. 'He's completely healed. I'm just so upset he didn't tell me how badly hurt he was! He still won't tell me exactly what happened.'

'Phoebe, he didn't want you to worry. You couldn't do anything for him, not when he was in the hospital in Australia,' Ada said.

'I know,' Phoebe said.

Henry came in with the drinks tray. This was the second weekend night we'd had drinks before dinner. When we'd first come to 'Two Trees' Phoebe only permitted cocktails on an occasional Friday night or a special occasion. And tonight there was a bottle of bourbon on the tray instead of sherry. I'd rather have had a Martini, prepared from the Gordon water I hid in my dresser drawer, but I accepted a tumbler of bourbon from Henry. I liked it, it went down smoothly. If my parents only knew how fond I'd become of a cocktail after work! I didn't know a soul in Wilmington who drank liquor, at least not in public.

Over the next few minutes Phoebe's color returned and she visibly pulled herself together, sitting up and smoothing her hair. 'Milt won't let me visit him in the hospital,' she said. 'He said some of the injuries on the ward are terrible and he doesn't want me to see them. I should be able to pick him up soon and bring him home to recuperate.'

'If his injuries were that serious he might not be sent overseas again,' Henry said, refreshing his glass of bourbon. 'He could be stationed here instead. You know, there's plenty of critical desk work to do.'

Ada and I couldn't help but glance at each other. Maybe it was selfish of us, but the housing situation in the District was a nightmare. It seemed that one of us would have to leave 'Two Trees'.

'I've been thinking, Phoebe,' Ada said. 'Milt can have my room. I have a friend I can stay with for a while.'

'Or I could sleep on the davenport,' I said. Which didn't solve the bathroom problem. Milt wouldn't want to share the second-floor bathroom with Ada and me. If he stayed at home more than a couple of weeks Ada and I might both have to move. The thought made me ill. I'd come to think of 'Two Trees' as my home. I knew Ada felt the same.

Phoebe shook her head firmly. 'No,' she said. 'Milt insists you keep your rooms. He's going to share Henry's space on the third floor. I have a plumber coming to install a shower and a real toilet in the box room.' Until now the men on the third floor had to make do with a chemical toilet and the bathtub in the basement next to the boiler. I wondered where Phoebe got the money for the renovation. Ada and I shared a glance of profound and grateful relief. I had a second bourbon. 'I'm looking forward to getting to know Milt,' Henry said. 'I want to hear all about his war experiences.'

Dinner that night was glorious beef! Hamburger steaks cooked medium rare with mushroom sauce, rice and salad made mostly from the greens in our garden. With fresh yeast rolls and real butter. And a honey cake. Dellaphine must have known we needed a decent meal and squandered our ration points. We'd pay for it later in the week with minced Spam croquettes.

I helped clear the table and as I stacked dishes near the sink for Dellaphine to wash, she whispered to me. 'Guess who is paying for the bathroom in the attic?' she asked.

'Who?'

'Mr Henry!'

'You're joking!'

'No, don't that beat all?'

'He's sweet on her, I've said it all along, haven't I, Momma?' Madeleine said. She'd come in late from work and was just now eating her dinner at the kitchen table.

'Yes, you did, honey,' Dellaphine said.

'And you pooh-poohed me.'

Dellaphine shook her head. 'I know. Now, Miss Phoebe said she would pay him back after the war when she cashed in her war bonds.'

'She won't need to if she marries him,' Madeleine said.

I was so incredulous I could hardly speak. Henry and Phoebe married! Surely not!

Dellaphine filled up the deep sink with hot water. Suds mountained up and she plunged her hands up over her elbows in it, scrubbing the dishes and pots and pans from dinner. I found a dishtowel and dried the dishes as she stacked them on the drainer.

Madeleine plunged her fork into her honey cake, scraping the plate with her fork to get every crumb.

'I swear,' Dellaphine said, 'if Miss Phoebe marries Mr Henry I'm leaving. Though I ain't worked or lived anywhere else but here.'

Madeleine brought her plate over to the sink. 'You can live with me, Momma,' she said, 'and retire. I'm going to get an apartment after the war.'

Dellaphine turned to her. 'Now don't you go thinking that way,' she said. 'All these jobs is going to go away after the war. Or the soldiers coming home, white men, will take them. Colored women won't be retiring or getting their own apartments in my lifetime.'

'Social Security isn't going away, Momma,' Madeleine said. 'And white men won't want to do my job.' She patted her mother on the arm and trotted down the steps to the room she shared with her mother on the daylight side of the basement.

'I worry about that girl,' Dellaphine said, her arms on her skinny hips as she watched her daughter go down the stairs. 'Her plans is too big, that's all there is to it.'

I worried too, but mainly about myself. Madeleine was right, Social Security wasn't going away after the war and men wouldn't want to type Social Security cards, not at a colored girl's salary. But my job was different. Would OSS even exist after the war? Would I be able to find work in the District? That reminded me of my parents' constant urging for me to find a second husband to support me. But the only man I was attracted to, one Joe Prager, I knew nothing at all about except the little that he told me, if that was the truth. And wouldn't he go home after the war, either to England or to Czechoslovakia? I didn't want to remarry just anyone who would have me to avoid moving back to my parents' house. I hadn't forgotten Dora Bertrand's promise to help me go to college after the war. Dora had a PhD in anthropology and taught at Smith. We had become friends when we worked in the same section. But since OSS had been reorganized I had seen her rarely. Would she still be eager to help me?

When I read women's magazines like *Good Housekeeping*, all the advertisements suggested women spend their war bonds after the war on homes, good china, furniture or a silver service. Assuming that all us working girls were going to set up housekeeping with a husband who'd pay the bills after the war. Me, I was more interested in my own apartment, a car or perhaps college.

I swear I would wait tables at Childs before I would go home to Wilmington and my childhood bedroom.

Detective Harvey Royal leaned up against a cherry tree to take the weight off his bad knee as he smoked a cigarette. He'd rounded up a couple of police officers to circle the Tidal Basin looking for any evidence that could be linked to his victim. If his victim had actually drowned in the Tidal Basin, then where was his hat? Every man over the age of eighteen in Washington wore a hat.

Royal had worked for the District Metropolitan Police for over forty years – he'd be retired now if it weren't for the war – and he'd not yet heard of an accident victim without anything in his pockets, even if it was only a pocket comb. The only reason for the victim to be stripped of his identification would be because he was murdered and the murderer wanted to hide the victim's identity as long as possible.

Had the corpse floated into the Tidal Basin from another watery location? The Tidal Basin was a reservoir that flushed the Washington Channel, the long harbor that separated the District from the fill lands of Potomac Park. The park contained two golf courses, a polo field and the grounds of the new Thomas Jefferson Memorial, all surrounded by hundreds of those damned pink trees.

The Basin's inlet gates, located on the Potomac, opened to admit water at high tide twice a day. The force of the water flow closed the outlet gates, which opened on to the Washington Channel. As the tide ebbed, the process reversed, keeping the Channel clear of high water and sediment. The gates were navigable and certainly wide enough to admit a floating body to the Tidal Basin. Royal just didn't think this was very likely. For one thing it had never happened before that he knew of.

One of his policemen bicycled up to him, then the other. They each had a bag of debris that had washed up on to the shores of the Basin. Royal instructed them to dump it all on the ground. Several single shoes, all small, probably children's shoes lost when children waded in the shallow part of the Basin. Lots of candy wrappers and empty cigarette packets. Two model sailboats, one quite large and new. Nothing that looked like it had belonged to their victim. Royal had hoped for a hat. That would prove that the victim had actually drowned in the Basin, not elsewhere.

'Thanks, boys,' Royal said. 'Go on back to the station. Put the sailboats in the lost and found and throw the rest away.'

After his men had cycled off Royal pulled copies of a photograph out of his jacket pocket. It was the least distressing photograph of the corpse that the police photographer had taken. It wasn't like he could do a house-to-house search for someone who might have known the victim, since there were no houses in the vicinity. But there must be some regulars in the area and he meant to find them.

He needed to take his car because of his knee so he climbed into the front seat and turned south for the short drive to the Jefferson Memorial.

The Memorial had only been open for a month. The statue inside was painted plaster. The final bronze statue would have to wait until after the war. A number of people were wandering around the open-air monument, and of course a few soldiers were guarding it.

Royal approached the ranking soldier, a corporal, and showed him his badge.

'Did you know a man's body was found in the Tidal Basin on Monday?' Royal asked him.

The corporal shifted his gun at ease. 'Yeah,' he said, 'I heard about that.'

'I'd like to show you a photo and see if you recognize him.'

'Sure,' the corporal said, 'but since the Memorial opened I've only been here twice.'

'Are there any regular guards; you know, people who are here every day?'

'Not really; our sergeant rotates our assignments all over the District.'

'Take a look at the picture anyway, would you?'

'Sure,' the soldier said, taking the picture from Royal.

'Man,' the soldier said, 'are you sure he drowned? That's quite a wallop he took on his head.'

'We don't know when he got it,' Royal said, 'but it sure could have helped him along.'

'Don't know him,' the soldier said. 'But I can take it back to my HQ and give it to my sergeant. He can make sure everyone gets a look at it.'

'That would be very helpful,' Royal said. 'Here's my card. If someone thinks he's seen this man, please have him call me.'

'Sure thing.'

Fat chance, Royal thought, resting his knee back in his car, that in a spot so teeming with people every day someone would recognize his victim. But there was one more place he might find an answer.

There was a streetcar terminus under the Bureau of Engraving and Printing just across the street from the Tidal Basin. The Pennsylvania Railroad coming from Virginia across the railroad bridge, or from the north through the District for that matter, had a stop there. From the terminus a person could get a streetcar or a bus anywhere in the city. Royal wondered if his victim was in the habit of making his connections at the streetcar terminus. And maybe taking his constitutional walking around the Tidal Basin.

Royal parked outside the Bureau of Engraving and Printing and walked down two flights of steps to the streetcar terminus. It functioned as a streetcar barn, too, but most of the cars were out.

For the rest of the day Royal met every streetcar that stopped and every driver who checked in at the office until the end of rush hour. Hundreds if not thousands of passengers passed by him. And every time he climbed aboard a car and showed the driver Hughes' picture, the response was pretty much the same. 'Sure I seen him, and a thousand of his twin brothers. All these guys look alike to me. You know how many times I've driven this route?'

At the end of the day Royal gave the terminus supervisor a copy of the victim's picture and his card with the request that the supervisor would post it in the drivers' lounge.

At seven thirty he knocked off. He stopped at a pub he knew well and ordered clam chowder and a grilled cheese sandwich. And a beer. He'd done all he could until the fingerprint girls at the FBI gave him a positive identification of the victim.

Rose Dudley lived in the Potomac House Apartments off 'I' Street on 25th, a long four blocks from my boarding house. The evening was lovely so I decided to go on foot, but I was winded from the walk and three flights of stairs when I finally knocked on Rose's apartment door. I hadn't known what to wear or whether I should bring food with me, so in the end I stayed in my work clothes and picked up a bag of Fritos at the Western Market on the way to Rose's apartment. Rose answered the door in a scarlet flowered kaftan that grazed the top of her bare feet. She had a cocktail in one hand and a celery stick heaped with pimento cheese in the other.

'Come in, dearie,' she said. 'Fritos! Yay! Sadie won't let me buy these, she says they're not healthy.' She looked at my demure suit with amusement. 'You are the picture of the conscientious government girl. What do you like to wear on the weekend?' she asked.

'Jeans and a sweater,' I said.

'Wear that the next time you come over. We don't believe that women should be forced to wear clothing they aren't comfortable in,' said a petite blonde woman with cropped hair who came into the room. She stuck out her hand. 'I'm Sadie,' she said, 'Rose's room-mate.' Sadie was comfortable in black leggings, a white shirt that hung below her fanny and a red scarf tied around her neck. She was drinking what appeared to be beer out of a Mason jar.

'Of course we must wear what our job dictates at work,' Sadie said. 'But not when we're in our own homes.'

'What's your poison, Louise?' Rose asked.

'Do you have any gin?' I asked.

'I'm drinking a gin sour myself. You want to try one?'

'I'd rather have a Martini if that's OK,' I said.

'Of course it is.'

'No olive, though, please,' I said.

'I'll just wave a little vermouth over it, shall I?' Rose said, parting a beaded curtain that hid a tiny kitchenette.

'Sit,' Sadie said to me, pointing to an upholstered chair with its back shaped like half a large keg. Dubiously I lowered myself into it and found it quite comfortable.

'What kind of chair is this?' I asked.

'A barrel chair,' Sadie said, draping herself over a matching chair and crossing her feet over a packing case that served as a coffee table.

Rose, trailing the hem of her flowered dress behind her, drifted back into the room with a tray and set it down on the trunk. It contained my Martini in a jelly jar, a bowl of Fritos and a carton of pimento cheese. She used the battered leather sofa between the chairs as a chaise, her bare feet crossed at the ankle across the arm of the sofa.

Sadie finished her beer and hopped up from her chair. 'Want to listen to some music?' she asked. 'What do you like?'

'Anything that's not Frank Sinatra!' Ada owned every Sinatra record and I could hear it from her room next door constantly. Not that the man didn't have a good voice. In fact I didn't much like crooners or big band music. Too mellow. I loved hillbilly music like The Carter Family and Roy Acuff, or Bob Wills. I was alone in my musical tastes in my boarding house. When I tuned the radio to the Grand Ole Opry on Saturday nights the lounge cleared out quickly. I didn't even think to suggest country music to Rose and Sadie. I could just imagine what they would think.

'Do you like jazz?' Sadie asked, flipping through a stack of twelve-inch seventy-eights that lay on the table where their record player sat.

Jazz was Negro music, though I knew lots of white people liked it and went to the colored nightclubs on the weekend to hear it. My only experience with jazz was the snatches I heard in the kitchen when Madeleine controlled the radio. Which wasn't often. Dellaphine usually changed the dial to a gospel station.

'I've not heard much jazz,' I said, 'but I'm willing to try it.'

'I've got lots of Duke Ellington,' Sadie said. 'He was born here in Washington, you know.'

We listened to 'Take the A Train', 'Cotton Tail', 'Stardust' and 'Jump for Joy' until it was time for seconds on our drinks. I liked jazz, I decided. It was loose and fun and had personality.

'I'm getting another gin sour,' Rose said, swinging her legs off the sofa. 'Another Martini?' she asked me.

'Sure,' I said.

As Rose vanished into the kitchen the apartment doorbell rang.

Sadie answered it and in breezed Peggy Benton.

'It's about time,' Sadie said. 'Where have you been?'

'I had to cook dinner and clean up,' Peggy said. 'Hi, Louise.'

'Hi,' I said.

'So now that your conjugal duties are completed satisfactorily you can come have a drink with your friends,' Rose said, coming out of the kitchen and handing me my Martini. 'I am never getting married. The usual, Peggy? Dubonnet on ice?'

'Please,' she said, 'and yes, Sadie, I had to feed my husband. But he's safely ensconced at his desk working now, just like every night.'

'It's a good thing your apartment house is just across our alley or we never would see you,' Sadie said.

Rose handed Peggy her tumbler of Dubonnet. Still a little breathless she dropped on to the sofa and sipped from it.

'What a day,' Peggy said. 'There is one piece of good news, though. Apparently Paul Hughes is OK. He was taken ill visiting his mother and since his landlady didn't have a telephone his mother sent a telegram.'

I perked up my ears.

'Paul is a friend of ours,' Rose said to me. 'He hasn't come to work this week and there was no word from him. We were all worried.'

'The office sent someone to Paul's boarding house and his landlady had gotten this telegram from Paul's mother. So I guess that he'll be back at work when he feels better,' Peggy said.

I didn't volunteer that I was that first 'someone', or that I had spent a day documenting Hughes' file usage at OSS.

'So, Sadie,' Rose said, 'what clever things did Mr Churchill say today?' She turned to me and said, 'Sadie is Terence Layman's secretary. She sees whatever crosses his desk.'

'You're joking,' I said. Layman was the most prominent gossip columnist in Washington. His column ran in the *Washington Times-Herald*, the conservative newspaper run by Cissy Patterson. Patterson loathed Roosevelt.

'Yes, I work for Mr Layman,' Sadie said. 'I don't agree with him politically, but I don't have to. I rarely see the man. He's out at parties most nights, comes into the office at all hours and leaves me instructions on the Dictaphone. The most interesting things cross his desk, you wouldn't believe. And no, Rose, I don't think Churchill said anything clever today.'

'You don't like Winston Churchill?' I asked.

Rose hooted.

'Of course not,' Peggy said, 'he's a Tory.'

'Although he makes an excellent speech, you have to admit,' Sadie said.

'That's just about his only positive trait,' Rose said.

I'd never before heard anyone speak about Prime Minister Churchill this way.

'Don't look so horrified, Louise,' Rose said. 'Oh, and don't worry, anything we talk about here doesn't leave this room.'

'So why don't you admire Churchill?' I asked.

'Let's see,' Sadie said, 'He's an aristocrat. And a royalist. You know, keep the servants in the basement just as God ordained it. Some people are simply born to be rich and powerful.'

'And the British Empire must keep its colonies. Like India. No matter how much the Indians want their freedom,' Rose said.

'Just wait until after the war is over,' Peggy said. 'I don't think speechifying will help Churchill much then. The British people will demand social reforms, not a return to feudalism.'

'I just hope life in this country doesn't revisit the thirties. Remember Herbert Hoover? Dear God,' Rose said.

I agreed with that.

'That does worry me,' I said. 'I want to keep working after the war is over. But will there be as many jobs for women?'

'Don't forget the Negroes,' Sadie said. 'After fighting in the war and working regular jobs do you think they're going to want to go back to sharecropping and cleaning houses?'

I thought of Madeleine. She wouldn't live her mother's life without putting up a fight.

'We're all going to have to work very hard to make sure that doesn't happen,' Sadie said.

'Which is why people like us have to meet and plan now,' Rose said. 'We must be prepared to act.'

I had been thinking much along the same lines. Worried about what would happen to me after the war. But I'd kept my thoughts to myself most of the time. It was liberating to talk openly to other girls who felt the same about the future as I did. Girls who did not want to go home to their parents or get married for marriage's sake after the war because there were no jobs for them. I felt a pang as I reminded myself that I'd avoided a romance with Joe to avoid offending anyone at OSS.

Peggy took a long sip of her Dubonnet. 'Gosh,' she said,

'this tastes so good.' She slid out of her light jacket and threw it on to the packing case which served as a coffee table. When it landed a pamphlet flew out of the pocket.

'Oh,' she said, 'I almost forgot! I picked up one of these at work. If you want to be outraged take a look.'

Rose reached for it. 'Listen to this,' she said, reading the title, '"Relocation of Japanese-Americans".' She read to herself for a few minutes. 'Disgraceful!' she said. 'The government is interning American citizens! A hundred thousand Japanese-Americans who've done absolutely nothing wrong at all!'

I noticed the publication line on the pamphlet: 'War Relocation Authority, May 1943'.

'Peggy, you didn't take that from work!' I said. 'You could be fired!'

Peggy shrugged. 'There were stacks of them,' she said. 'No one will miss one. I figured Sadie could take it to her boss and perhaps he'd write an article about it.'

Sadie hooted. 'Not a chance; he works for the *Herald*, remember?' she said. 'But I know a cub reporter for the *Post* I can slip it to.'

'Don't look so horrified,' Peggy said to me. 'The pamphlet is being routed to the Library of Congress and bunches of other places. It's not secret.' She picked it up and tossed it to me. I could only bear to read the first paragraph.

'. . . with invasion of the west coast looming as an imminent possibility, the Western Defense Command of the United States Army decided that the military situation required the removal of all persons of Japanese ancestry from a broad coastal strip. In the weeks that followed, both American-born and alien Japanese residents were moved from a prescribed zone comprising the entire State of California, the western half of Oregon and Washington, and the southern third of Arizona', I read. What military situation, I wondered? Did the military really think that if Japan invaded the west coast Japanese-Americans would join them? What about the Japanese military dictatorship would appeal to them? It was absurd. I felt sick.

'I need another drink,' Rose said, lifting herself from the sofa and heading toward a makeshift bar.

My God, I thought. Innocent Americans from four states imprisoned without due process. For once I couldn't keep my mouth shut. 'Of course,' I said, after browsing the rest of the pamphlet, 'the internment camps have all the comforts of home, behind their barbed wire fences.' I tossed the pamphlet to Sadie. I didn't think it would matter much if she could find a reporter to write the story. Most Americans agreed with the government's internment policies. I did too, once.

As I walked home from Rose's place in the soft spring evening I felt as tranquil as I'd been in ages. I'd spent the evening with women like me . . . well, Rose and Sadie were more radical than me, but still we were simpatico much of the time. Where I could actually say out loud much of what I thought without Henry or Phoebe tut-tutting me. And have a cocktail in a lounge instead of in my bedroom. And listen to new music instead of the same old big band stuff.

'I hope you'll come back next week,' Rose had said as she walked me to the entrance of her apartment house.

'I'll be here,' I said. Next time I'd bring a bottle of gin with me to restock the bar.

As I turned into the front gate of 'Two Trees' Ada came out of the house, shutting the door softly behind her.

'Hi,' I said, surprised to see her.

She raised her finger to her lips and hurried up to me, taking my arm and leading me back out to the sidewalk.

'What on earth—' I began.

'Shhh,' she whispered. 'Come, we need to stand where we can't be seen from the lounge.'

We moved down the street a few yards. 'What is it?' I asked. 'What's wrong?'

'It's Milt,' she said. 'Oh, Louise, it's terrible. Awful.'

'Why?' I said.

'He was badly hurt. Much worse than he told Phoebe. She

got the phone call from the hospital right after you left and she and Henry went to pick Milt up. He's gotten so drunk since he got home. You need to be prepared to meet him.'

'What happened to him?' I asked, afraid of the answer.

The door to 'Two Trees' opened.

'Louise,' Phoebe called out, 'I thought I heard your voice. Come inside and meet my son!'

Ada squeezed my arm hard. 'I need to find a taxi and get to the hotel. I'm playing ten to two tonight.' She hurried down the street toward Pennsylvania Avenue.

I found myself inside the entrance hall of 'Two Trees', being led by Phoebe into the lounge where Henry and Milt sat. At first I didn't notice anything, but then Milt stood up. His left shirtsleeve was neatly rolled up and pinned under his shoulder. He was missing his entire left arm.

Thanks to Ada's warning I was able to react without shock.

'Louise,' Phoebe said, 'this is my oldest son, Milt.'

Milt stood up, swaying slightly, and extended his right hand.

'So you are the delightful Louise,' he said. 'I'm pleased to meet you.'

I shook his hand firmly. 'I'm glad to meet you, too, and happy that you're home safely.'

I didn't want to pretend I didn't notice his injury. 'I hope you're recovering well,' I said.

Milt picked up a glass from the table as he sat down, draining the inch or so of bourbon left in it. 'With some help from my friend here,' he said, tossing the glass back. 'I'd like another, please, Mother.'

Phoebe poured him another shot, her hands shaking slightly. Henry, sitting across from Milt, hadn't said a word yet and clutched his own glass.

I took a deep breath and sat down next to Milt on the sofa. 'I'm so sorry about your injury,' I said.

'You don't need to be,' he said. 'It's just part of the job of being a hero.' He drained his bourbon in one gulp.

Henry's lips tightened into a thin line.

THREE

General experience indicates that "husky" girls—those who are just a little on the heavy side—are likely to be more even-tempered and efficient than their underweight sisters.

'1943 Guide to Hiring Women', *Mass Transportation* magazine, July 1943.

With a little trepidation I got off the bus at New Hampshire and 'U' Street, right in the middle of the colored neighborhood of Washington. It was teeming with people as I expected it would be on Saturday night. Throngs of Negroes wearing everything from zoot suits to military uniforms to tuxedos crowded the streets on their way to 'U' Street's famous bars and clubs. Plenty of white people strolled 'U' Street, too, lured there by hot music, especially jazz, the best in the country outside of Harlem.

Which is why I was there.

At lunch on Friday Rose slid into a spot next to me at the cafeteria table where I was eating chicken à la king with Joan. 'Louise,' she said, 'Sadie and I have decided we are going to "U" Street on Saturday night to see what all the excitement is about. Don't you want to come with us?'

'"U" Street?' Joan said. 'At night? Do you think that's a good idea?'

Rose shrugged. 'Why not?' she said. 'Just because it's a colored neighborhood doesn't mean it's not safe.'

'I didn't mean that,' Joan said. 'It's just that so many of the nice hotels have jazz bands now; why not go to the Willard or the Mayflower?'

'I've been to the Willard and the Mayflower,' I said. 'I've never been to "U" Street.'

'I've heard there's sometimes gunfire in the streets and police raids on those clubs,' Joan said.

Rose ignored her and said to me, 'Guess who's playing at the Club Bali! Louis Armstrong and his orchestra!'

The Club Bali. I'd seen its advertisements, bordered in palm fronds and strewn with exclamation points, in the newspaper almost every day ('In Person! On Stage!'). It was the biggest club in the 'U' Street neighborhood and served exotic Korean food. I'd never dreamed of going to such a place before.

'I'd love to come,' I said.

'It's expensive,' Rose said. 'The cover charge is five dollars, dinner about two fifty or so, and then there'll be the drinks.'

'I'll cash a check on my way home,' I said. I could skip buying a war bond this month.

'First one who gets there saves a table,' Rose said. 'For four. We're going to bring a man friend with us to chaperone. See, Joan, we can be proper!'

For a minute it looked like Joan was going to ask to go with us. I could see in her expression that her fun-loving nature was struggling with her lofty upbringing, but in the end she gave in to the upbringing.

After Rose left Joan said to me, 'Be careful and call me Sunday. I want to hear all about it.'

I escaped the bustle of 'U' Street, turning off on to 14th and walking south to 'T', where the crowds were less stifling. A long line of colored and white people stood outside the entrance to the Club Bali, where two bouncers at the door made sure no one was carrying guns or their own liquor. Once inside the men checked their hats in the cloakroom. I paid my five dollars and moved with the crowd into the main room. It was huge and filling up fast. I guessed the space could hold almost three hundred people. A raised stage topped with a phoney thatched roof jutted from the far wall. The band playing on it was just an opening act, I guess, no one was paying any attention to the singer and I didn't recognize the music. Plastic palm trees with red paper flowers tied to them lined the dance floor. Pretty colored girls in grass skirts with trays hanging around their necks worked the crowd, offering mementos for sale as well as cigarettes. Already a few people were eating at tables that hardly looked big enough to hold one plate. The odor of the Korean food was foreign to me, but I could hardly wait to taste it.

I spotted Sadie waving at me from a table near a corner of the stage. I edged my way to it between the crowded tables and squeezed into a chair. Rose was there too, and a tallish man wearing a blue linen suit stood to be introduced to me. I recognized him immediately. He was Clark Leach, one of General Donovan's most trusted aides. Leach was an expert on China and spoke fluent Mandarin, sometimes even translating for the President. He was one of the Yale-educated crowd that filled so many spots at OSS. I guessed he was about forty. His dark hair was greying at the temples and receding a bit. Eyeglasses protruded from his handkerchief pocket.

'This is our friend Mrs Louise Pearlie,' Rose said to him.

'Pleased to meet you, I'm Clark Leach,' he said. I shook his outstretched hand.

'Call me Louise, please,' I said.

'And I'm Clark,' he answered.

I didn't expect Leach to recognize me from OSS. He was a star while I was just another government girl. So of course I wouldn't indicate that I knew he worked at OSS.

'We ordered food for you, I hope that was OK,' Sadie said to me.

'That's fine,' I said. 'I wouldn't know what to get anyway.'

'Clark steered us away from too much spice,' Rose said. 'We figured we'd share everything.'

An exotic-looking mulatto waitress with an order pad stopped by our table. She wore a sarong and a top that was more like a bra, except that it was patterned with flowers. Real flowers – orchids, I thought – decorated her long soft black hair. 'Ready for drinks?' she asked.

'Start a tab for me,' Clark said. 'I'll take care of the drinks.'

'No, Clark,' Sadie said, 'you mustn't, we can pay for our own drinks.'

Clark shook his head. 'You've had me over to your apartment so many times for drink and food this is the least I can do. I'll have bourbon, on ice,' he said to the barmaid.

'I'll have a gin sour,' Rose said. I requested my usual dry Martini without olives and Sadie ordered a beer.

'Clark is one of those rare men who appreciates intelligent women,' Rose said.

'You sell our sex short,' Clark said. 'Many men like smart women. And I'm not perfect. I enjoy the company of attractive women too. Tonight I am fortunate to be with ladies who have both attributes.'

'We're not blotto enough to fall for that line, Clark,' Sadie said. 'Not yet, anyway.'

Clark smiled a friendly, familiar smile at Rose and Sadie, and I found myself thinking that if Rose and Sadie were fond of him he was bound to be OK. And I was glad I looked nice tonight. I'd worn a black and white striped rayon dress with sleeves that stopped above my elbows, a thin black belt, my pearls and an artificial but darling white flower pinned gaily behind one ear. Festive, but still in good taste, I hoped.

The waitress returned with a tray crowded to its edge with drinks and passed ours across the table to us. My Martini had an olive in it but I didn't care because it was pierced with a fancy pink toothpick. I discarded the olive and put the stick in my purse as a souvenir. I sipped my Martini slowly. If we were going to be here for hours I didn't want to drink too much.

The opening band finished their set and left the stage to a scattering of applause. An emcee with slicked back, glistening hair and a wide-lapel tuxedo stepped on to the stage and grasped the microphone. Anticipation rippled through the audience.

'Welcome,' the emcee said, 'to the Club Bali! I'm not going to waste your time, my friends! Tonight we have here on our stage, live, one of our favorite performers, Louis Armstrong!'

The roar from the crowd made me cover my ears. Armstrong, followed by his band, strolled on to the stage. It was a big band. The musicians had to squeeze themselves and their instruments into their places. Armstrong, his cornet tucked under his arm, grasped the microphone.

'Ladies and gentlemen of our great nation's capital, I am honored to be here!' When he said the word 'honored' he tossed his head back and smiled, showing bright white teeth in a wide mouth. He turned to his orchestra. 'Are you boys ready?' he asked.

'We're ready!' they answered in unison.

Armstrong let go of the mike and swiveled, raising his right hand to conduct his band. The band broke into 'Heebie Jeebies', and if I had the rest of my life I'd never be able to describe it. It wasn't sparse and structured like hillbilly music, not mellow and organized like swing, it was loose and happy. Every instrument spoke independently but somehow as part of a whole piece. The music felt and sounded free. From there the band played 'Alexander's Ragtime Band' and 'Standing on the Corner'. Armstrong's cornet was clear and true but I think I liked his singing even better. No one would say he had a good voice, nothing like Sinatra or Bing Crosby, but its raspiness gave his songs a personality no one could imitate. After he sang 'Dinah' with a touch of scat I didn't see how anyone else could do it better.

Clark reached out a hand to me. 'Dance?' he said.

'Yes, please.'

We edged out on to the crowded floor.

'I'm sorry, but I can only foxtrot,' Clark said.

'Thank God,' I said.

As men and women gyrated around us Clark put his hand around my waist and took my hand. He didn't pull me right up to him. It was all quite seemly. Clark's foxtrot was smooth, even if it was the only dance he could do. We couldn't talk, it was just too noisy. We stayed on the floor dancing to a few more tunes. One called 'Potato Head Blues' made me want to break loose from Clark's foxtrot and lindy-hop. But I managed to restrain myself for Clark's sake. There was a shortage of men so Sadie and Rose jitterbugged together.

After the set ended Armstrong wiped the sweat from his face with a huge white handkerchief and said, 'Just a little break now, y'all. Enjoy your dinner!' He and the band left the stage to a cacophony of applause and cheers.

'What a swell sound!' Sadie said, as she took her seat again.

'What do you think?' Clark asked me.

'I thought he was grand!' I said.

'He's a great talent,' Leach said. 'I wish Billie Holiday was here with him tonight. Then you would hear some singing!'

'You've seen Billie Holiday?' I asked.

'Before the war, when I lived in New York City, I used to go the Savoy Ballroom with friends all the time.'

'In Harlem? What was it like?'

'It reminded me of Paris. The streets were jammed with people, all kinds of people from every walk of life, enjoying life, food, music, fun. Americans can be such damn puritans.'

Sadie leaned into the conversation and lowered her voice. 'Don't they let colored people and white people dance together at the Savoy?'

'Yes they do,' Clark answered. 'Like Paris. Before the war.' His face darkened. 'That bastard Hitler.'

During the heavy pause that followed a waiter brought us our dinner. A good thing, too; I'd let my friends convince me to order another Martini and my head was buzzing.

Clark had selected four dishes for us to share. There was a fried rice dish mounded with vegetables and an egg, chicken teriyaki, chicken dumplings and a noodle dish he said was quite spicy.

'Watch out for the chillies,' Clark said, pointing out the thin red strips embedded in the noodles. Even avoiding the chillies I had to drink half of Sadie's beer to cool my mouth.

The food was delicious, if unfamiliar, and I ate my fair share.

After the table was cleared Sadie and Rose convinced me to order another Martini.

'There's another set to go,' Rose said. 'Plenty of time for the buzz to wear off.'

Armstrong and his band walked out on stage again and the audience stood up in unison and roared. He launched into 'Summertime' but instead of music I heard a distant roaring in my head and my legs trembled. My dinner began to roil in my stomach and I sat down hard. I was suddenly conscious of the wafting clouds of cigarette smoke that filled the room. It stung my eyes and made my throat ache.

Sadie sat down next to me and took my arm. 'Are you all right?' she asked.

'I don't feel well,' I said.

'Let's get you some water,' Rose said.

'Don't let me faint in front of all these people,' I said.

In a second Clark was by my side. 'I'll take you outside for some air,' he said. 'There's a back garden. We'll get you some water out there.' He pulled me up from my seat and put an arm around my waist to support me. I gripped his shoulder. 'Come on,' he said, 'it's just a few steps.'

He guided me out a back door and into a rear garden where few of the tables were taken.

The garden was ringed with trees strung with glowing light bulbs and the air was cool, at least compared to the air inside.

Clark settled me in a chair. I inhaled huge gulps of air as if I'd been drowning. Clark beckoned for the waitress who served the garden.

'Can you get the lady a glass of cold water?' he asked. 'And bring a pitcher more, with ice.'

The waitress took one look at me and said, 'Ma'am, would you like some Bromo-Seltzer in your glass of water?'

'Yes, please,' I said. Unconsciously I placed a hand on my churning stomach.

'I'm so sorry,' Clark said. 'I should have been more careful ordering dinner.'

'I don't think it was the food,' I said. 'I blame the third Martini. Thanks for bringing me outside. If I'd collapsed in there I'd have been mortified.'

'No worries. It's lovely out here.'

The waitress brought me my Bromo-Seltzer fizzing in a tall glass, and a pitcher of water.

After I'd swallowed the Bromo I felt much better. I chased it with a glass of pure, cold water.

'Better?' Clark asked.

'Much,' I said. 'Please go back inside. I don't want you to miss the show. I'm fine out here.'

'I'd rather stay with you. We can still hear the music.'

We could. The sound rose and fell with the slight breeze that drifted through the garden.

There were just two other couples outside. They were tables away from us.

Clark leaned closer to me and lowered his voice. 'No one can hear us, Louise,' he said. 'I believe we work for the same agency? I've seen you in the Registry many times.'

I nodded. 'I know who you are, of course.'

'What's your clearance?' he asked.

I waited until the waitress passed by, then answered. 'Top Secret.'

Clark nodded. 'I thought so. Aren't you the woman who—'

'Yes,' I said quickly. 'That's me. But I don't think we should talk about it.'

'You're correct, of course. But I can tell you all about what I'm doing. It's not one bit confidential.'

'What then?' I asked.

'Every day I pick up Dr T.V. Soong from the Chinese Embassy and drive him to the Federal Reserve Building, where they're holding the Trident Conference, and stay by his side all day. His English is excellent of course, but he likes to speak Chinese to me, and I take notes for him.'

Soong was Foreign Minister of China and brother-in-law to both Dr Sun Yat-sen and Generalissimo Chiang Kai-shek. He was a wealthy banker who financed the Flying Tigers before they became part of the US Air Force.

'He's the only delegate from China,' Clark continued. He glanced around the garden to make sure no one was near. 'And there's no representative from the Soviet Union. Do you believe that? The Russians have withstood Stalingrad and continue to engage Germany on the Eastern Front, yet they weren't invited to help plan the next phase of the war?'

The next phase of the war was a future cross-channel invasion of Europe. Oh, I could chat knowledgeably about the issues being discussed at Trident, but I had no intention of doing so. It was fine for Clark to expound all he wanted about politics and his work at OSS, he had the pay grade, but I was just a government girl, and I wasn't about to engage him in policy discussions. If I took one step too far in our conversation he might take umbrage and then I would be in trouble.

I took a sip of water. 'Perhaps we should go back inside?'

Clark grinned at me. 'Smart woman,' he said. 'You're right, I should be more reserved in public. Guess I had a little too much to drink myself. Do you really want to go back inside?'

'Actually, no,' I said. 'I've had a wonderful time, but I think I should be heading home.'

'Let me take you,' he said. 'I have my car.'

'That's all right, I came on the bus.'

'I'm taking Sadie and Rose back to their apartment; I can drop you off with no trouble.'

'Are they ready to leave?'

'Let me go ask them.'

I was surprised that Clark Leach had spoken to me so freely, but there was no one within earshot and nothing he'd said was remotely secret or confidential. I took out my lipstick and compact and tried to bring a little color back into my face.

Clark appeared with Sadie and Rose in tow.

'That was fun,' Sadie said. 'But I'm tuckered out!'

'They'll keep partying for hours,' Rose said. 'Until morning probably.'

'I suppose you have to work up to clubbing, like doing a hundred push-ups,' Clark said. 'We can get out this gate here, I think. My car should be down the street about a block.'

Clark's car was a roomy Buick with luscious white upholstery and a mahogany dashboard. He must have a private income; he couldn't afford a car like that on a government salary. Most of the big men in OSS were 'dollar a year' men, like General Donovan and my own boss, Wilmarth Lewis. I sat in front while Sadie and Rose climbed in back.

'Let's go again next week,' Sadie said.

'I'll have to save up,' Rose said. 'It's expensive.'

'That's how they get the best clientele,' Clark said. 'Colored or white, a five-dollar cover charge is a lot of money.'

'Thank you for the drinks, Clark,' I said. 'I'm not as broke as I might be otherwise.'

'You're welcome,' he said. 'It was a pleasure.'

Clark dropped Sadie and Rose off first. I was worried that he might use the opportunity to ask me out on a date. Like I thought earlier, his pay grade was way above mine. To my relief he didn't.

'Don't come around,' I said, opening my car door myself in front of my boarding house. I wanted to keep him at arm's length.

'Will I see you at Sadie and Rose's next week?' he asked.

'Absolutely,' I said. I planned to come to their 'salon' every Thursday as long as they'd have me. I could talk to Sadie and Rose in a way I couldn't speak to anyone else in Washington. Plus I had to get a look at Paul Hughes, whose bout of the flu at his mother's house had caused so much fuss.

I told myself that I didn't have a hangover. I had a shocking headache because of the clouds of cigarette smoke in the Club Bali, not the three Martinis I'd slurped. And my stomach lurched on account of the exotic Korean food, not because of the three Martinis either.

I put on my glasses and staggered into the bathroom, where I washed my face and brushed my teeth. I don't think I had ever seen my eyes bloodshot before. It did not improve my appearance. Neither did the dark circles below my eyes that made me look like a raccoon. I pulled my stringy hair back in a bun. I could smell the smoke of a hundred cigarettes still clinging to my body. I wanted desperately to bathe but I needed to put something in my stomach first.

Back in my bedroom I dressed in jeans and my favorite blue and buff George Washington University sweatshirt. I swear I tiptoed going down the stairs to avoid the noise of my footsteps. And I gripped the stair banister as though falling was imminent. Never again, I swore. Now I knew my limit. No more than two Martinis in one evening!

Milt must have slept late too. He sat alone at the kitchen table eating pancakes, cutting them with the edge of his fork.

''Morning,' he said. 'You look like you had fun last night.'

'I did,' I said. 'I think. Who fixed the pancakes?' Dellaphine didn't cook breakfast or supper on Sundays. She poured all her energies into Sunday dinner when she got home from the Gethsemane Baptist Church.

'Henry,' Milt said. 'They're real good.' He gestured with his fork toward the range.

'Want some? There're plenty left. Not a lot of maple syrup though. Fresh coffee too.'

My stomach lurched and it must have shown on my face.

'Maybe not,' Milt said.

'I'm going to fix some toast,' I said. Dry toast. Washed down with plain water, with maybe some more Bromo-Seltzer in it.

'Where did you go last night?' Milt asked. 'No, sorry, it's none of my business.'

'I don't mind. The Club Bali.'

Milt forked the last bite of pancake into his mouth before he spoke.

'No joke! That's in the colored part of town. "U" Street, right?'

'Just around the corner. It was grand. "Satchmo" Armstrong played. And we had Korean food.'

'Slant-eye food? I'm surprised the club could get away with that.'

'Korean isn't the same as Japanese.'

Milt shrugged, laying down his fork before picking up his coffee cup.

'They all look the same,' he said. 'There are plenty of Koreans in the Japanese Imperial Army.'

Korea had been occupied by the Japanese and its citizens conscripted into the Japanese Army and into labor camps in Japan. Instead of arguing with Milt, who after all had lost an arm and was bound to hate the Japs and anyone who fought alongside them, I went into Dellaphine's pantry to find the Bromo-Seltzer.

But Milt wasn't done. 'They should fire that Korean cook, and throw him into an internment camp.' He could see from my expression when I went back into the kitchen that I didn't appreciate what he'd said. 'Shocked?' he said. He nodded at his empty sleeve. 'Better yet, send the lot of them back where they came from in boxes.'

'I'm sorry about your arm, Milt,' I said. 'Terribly sorry. I can't imagine what you've been through. But George Kim didn't wound you. He came to this country to escape from the Japanese.'

Before I said anything more to Milt that I might regret later – he was my landlady's son, after all –I went upstairs to bathe. I felt like I was washing more than smoke off myself. I'd been wrong about Milt and Henry sharing a room. It looked like they'd get along real well.

I rose out from beneath my covers feeling like Lazarus. I couldn't remember the last time I'd taken a nap. My headache was gone, my stomach was quiet and I thought I would live.

I'd fallen asleep after my bath in my underwear, wrapped up in a blanket. I recalled that I'd just planned to rest for a few minutes.

Then I heard the pounding on my door.

'For heaven's sake, come in!' I said. 'There's no reason to break the door down.'

Ada opened the door.

'You're alive, good,' she said. 'I've been taking messages for you all afternoon. Joan has called you three times. A man called too. And you missed Sunday dinner. Don't you think you should get up?'

'What time is it?' I asked.

'Four o'clock,' she said.

'I'm coming.' Joan would want to know all about the Club Bali and I was starving.

I hoped there were leftovers from Sunday dinner in the refrigerator. I could always scramble some eggs. I threw off my covers.

'I'll be down in a minute.'

Ada sat on my bed to wait while I dressed. She wore black capris, a pink cable knit sweater and straw espadrilles. Her peroxide hair was swathed in a matching pink turban.

'Don't you want to know about the man who called?'

'Sure,' I said, pulling on the same jeans and sweatshirt I'd worn down to breakfast.

'Did he leave his name?'

'Clark Leach,' she said.

'Oh.' I checked my mirror. I'd slept on my wet hair. I looked like a witch. Brushing it back tight I secured it into a ponytail.

'Not interested?'

'He's not calling me for a date. He's way out of my league,' I said. 'He went with us to the club last night. I had too much to drink.'

'He probably thinks you're fast,' she said, teasing me. She pulled her cigarette holder out from behind an ear. 'I'm going to go out on the porch and have a cigarette. Please call Joan. That girl really wants to talk to you.'

I spent fifteen minutes telling Joan everything that had happened at the Club Bali.

'I was a fool not to go,' she said.

'You can come with us the next time,' I said. 'It will be a while for me. It's not cheap.'

'By the way,' she said. 'Have you read the paper yet?'

'Not yet.' I was eager to get her off the line. My stomach was growling.

'One of our people drowned in the Tidal Basin. Did you know him? His name was Paul Hughes.'

FOUR

Retain a physician to give each woman you hire a special
physical examination—one covering female conditions.
This step not only protects the property against the possibility
of lawsuit but also reveals whether the employee-to-be
has any female weaknesses which would make her
mentally or physically unfit for the job.

'1943 Guide to Hiring Women', *Mass Transportation*
magazine, July 1943.

My hunger forgotten for the time being, I rummaged
through the *Washington Post* looking for the story
on Paul Hughes' death. I found it in the local section
well below the fold. I read the story twice, trying to fit the
reporter's chronology of events into mine. Hughes' corpse
had been found Monday by a soldier patrolling the shores
of the Tidal Basin. By Friday his fingerprints had identified
him as Paul Hughes, a mid-level government employee. That
in itself seemed odd to me – didn't Hughes have his wallet
on him? According to Hughes' landlady, who was in tears
when the reporter talked to her, Hughes had fallen ill with
the flu while visiting his mother in Fredericksburg. A
spokesman for Hughes' employer, of course not identified
as OSS, said that the police investigation concluded that
Hughes returned by train to the District on Sunday, despite
what his mother had said in her telegram. Apparently still
weak from his illness, Hughes must have fainted while
walking from the train station to the streetcar terminal underneath the Bureau of Engraving on the path around the Tidal
Basin. The police could only speculate that he hit his head
on the rocks that lined the shore of the Tidal Basin, fell
in and drowned. A freak accident, they called it. Very

unfortunate. He was a popular and competent employee. All sympathies to his family and friends.

That meant that when I checked into Hughes' file use on Tuesday, when I visited Mrs Nighy on Wednesday, Hughes was already dead. Tucked into a refrigerated drawer at the District police morgue until his fingerprints were identified.

I poured a cup of coffee and carried it and the section of the *Post* I was reading up to my bedroom, where I added sugar to the coffee cup from the dwindling pound I'd bought on the black market a couple of months ago. OK, so I wasn't a perfect American patriot. But there were far worse violators of the ration rules than me. Take Henry, now. Last winter he'd stocked the garage with jerry cans of black market gasoline he'd bought somewhere. And driving Phoebe's car, fueled by that illegal gas, he'd criss-crossed the Virginia countryside in search of an illegal source for prime beef. He justified himself by explaining that rationing was illegal under the Constitution, and besides, Roosevelt just didn't understand the concept of supply and demand. Phoebe had finally insisted that Henry stop violating the Office of Price Protection regulations, afraid he would get caught and she might be in trouble for not reporting him.

I was a curious person. Too curious, my parents used to say. Paul Hughes' story fascinated me, so I climbed on to my bed with a notebook and a pencil to lay out the chronology of the week's events.

The last time anyone at OSS had seen Paul Hughes was Friday at the end of the workday. This was confirmed by Don Murray, my old boss, who now worked in Hughes' division as Assistant Head. According to his landlady, Hughes went to Fredericksburg on that Friday after work to visit his mother. He didn't take a suitcase, as he kept spare clothes and toiletries at his mother's.

Sunday Mrs Nighy got a telegram from Hughes' mother saying he was ill and wouldn't return to the District until he'd recovered. Mrs Nighy didn't have either an address or a telephone number for Hughes' mother. Monday Hughes didn't show up for work. On Tuesday Major Wicker assigned me to find out what files Hughes had been reading, with no explanation, except that it was a convenient time as Hughes was absent. After I turned in my notes I was dismissed until Wicker asked me to go to Hughes' boarding house to inquire after him. That was on Wednesday.

When I visited Hughes' landlady she gave me the telegram from Hughes' mother telling her that he was ill. There was no way that OSS could have been notified. Neither Mrs Nighy nor Hughes' mother would know that Hughes worked for OSS. No OSS employee would give out that information – no one in my boarding house knew I worked there. Joe had guessed but we never discussed it. You would think that Hughes would have thought of some way to notify his office that he was ill. Unless he was so ill he just couldn't. But then why did he return to the District on Sunday after his mother sent that telegram?

On the east side of the Tidal Basin, the streetcar terminus underneath the Bureau of Engraving and the railroad stop just where the Railway Bridge entered the District were just footsteps away from each other. Hughes could have disembarked from a northbound Virginia train and walked a section of the Tidal Basin path to reach the streetcar stop. From there he could hop a streetcar to Foggy Bottom and his rooming house.

Then there was the note Hughes had scribbled at his desk. About meeting one 'G' on Sunday. I had assumed this meeting was to happen in Fredericksburg, since I thought he had gone to his mother's there. Now I wondered if Hughes had returned to the District to make that meeting with 'G'.

And I could swear that on Thursday, when I went to Rose's apartment, Peggy Benton said Hughes was coming back to work as soon as he was well. Don Murray had said much the same thing when I talked to him. I had assumed that OSS had somehow checked up on Hughes, but maybe not. Perhaps Major Wicker and Don Murray had simply taken Hughes' mother's telegram at face value and assumed that Hughes would return to work as soon as he was well. I mean, why wouldn't they? With the Trident Conference on, OSS had enough to do without worrying about a sick employee.

What I couldn't figure out was why Hughes wasn't identified until after his fingerprints were processed. Didn't the man have his wallet on him? And who the hell was 'G'? Was 'G' an old friend Hughes intended to meet for drinks? Or a contact related to his job at OSS? And why did Major Wicker want me to check on the files Hughes was reading?

None of this was any of my business, but I loathed loose ends that refused to tie themselves into a neat bow.

'Louise!' Ada hollered up the stairs to me. 'Telephone again, for God's sake!'

For one brief thrilling second I thought it might be Joe. But it couldn't be. It was too expensive to call long distance. And I remembered, with a deep pang of guilt, that I hadn't written him back after receiving his letter on Tuesday. I had to write him tonight. But just the thought of putting my thoughts on paper made me feel terribly lonely. I almost wanted to avoid that depth of feeling by not writing. But he'd wonder why he hadn't heard from me and I couldn't bear to cause him any unhappiness.

'Coming!' I answered. Shoving the newspaper section and my notebook into the top drawer of my dresser I ran down the stairs to get the telephone.

'Honestly,' Ada said, handing me the receiver, 'you'd think I was your secretary!'

It was Clark Leach.

'Louise,' Clark said, 'I'm calling to find out if you're feeling OK? Your friend said you were napping earlier.'

'I'm fine,' I said. 'I ate and drank too much last night, that's all.'

'But you had fun?'

'Oh, yes,' I said.

I heard voices in the lounge, so I stuck my head in to be polite and greet my housemates before I went hunting for leftovers in the kitchen.

Phoebe and Milt sat together on the davenport. Milt still

wore his pajamas and held a tumbler of bourbon and ice in his only hand. The bourbon bottle on the coffee table was less than half full. Henry was seated on the matching armchair, or it used to match before Phoebe threw a crocheted bedspread over it to hide the worn spots. Ada and I had been plotting to slipcover the lounge set for her – we knew its shabbiness embarrassed her – but we hadn't found enough good fabric at the right price yet.

'Hi, Louise,' Henry said. 'I'm trying to convince Milt and Phoebe to let me take them out to supper.'

'I don't want to go out in public,' Milt said. 'Besides, I'm not hungry.' He took a swallow from his drink. 'I had plenty at dinner.'

'Dear,' Phoebe said, 'I could fix you some scrambled eggs.' She drew a lap robe further up Milt's body. Milt pushed her hand away roughly. 'Don't, Mother, it's too hot,' he said. Phoebe replaced her trembling hand in her lap.

'Milt just needs more time to recuperate,' Phoebe said to Henry. 'He's had such an awful time.'

Milt poured himself another drink.

Henry shrugged. 'Sure,' he said, 'of course. Anyone else want to go out to eat with me? Phoebe?'

She shook her head. 'I'm not hungry either.'

'OK,' he said. 'I'm off then. I won't be late.' He left and I heard the door close behind him.

'I'm going on upstairs,' Milt said. 'I'm tired.'

'Oh, honey, please don't,' Phoebe said. 'Sunday nights we all gather here and have popcorn and listen to Walter Winchell.'

'I want to be alone,' Milt said, dumping the lap blanket on the floor as he stood up. 'I have my own radio.'

After he left the room Phoebe turned to me, hands twisting in her lap. 'I just don't know what to do,' she said. 'Milt's so unhappy.'

'I don't think there's much anyone can do, until he makes peace with losing his arm,' I said.

'But it's all so awful. He thinks his life is ruined.'

I'd grown up in Wilmington, North Carolina where men made their living fishing the open ocean and building ships. It was a rough and dangerous life. Men drowned, dragged off their boats when their nets tangled around them. They fell off scaffolding in the boatyards. Or had legs amputated when they were caught in canning machinery. I was used to seeing men, and some women, who'd lost fingers, or an arm or a leg. As long as I could remember, one of my daddy's workmen, who shucked oysters, picked crab and cleaned bluefish, limped around on a peg leg. No one thought anything of it.

But Milt was a college boy and from the city to boot. Good-looking, young, destined for a job in banking or some such profession, the possibility that he'd go though his life without an arm hadn't occurred to him. And he wouldn't have had any example of surviving a terrible injury and adjusting to it. He didn't yet appreciate that he was lucky to be alive.

Enough of Milt. He wasn't my problem. I was hungry. Back in the kitchen I ran into Madeleine foraging in the refrigerator. Dellaphine, on her regular Sunday night off, was enjoying a potluck supper at her church and visiting with her friends. Together Madeleine and I heated up leftover fried chicken, butter beans and mashed potatoes. We sat together at the kitchen table to eat. Phoebe would have preferred that I sit at the dining-room table by myself, but I was a poor Southerner, not a rich one, and I was used to living and working in close quarters with colored people.

'Miss Ada said you went to the Club Bali last night,' Madeleine said. 'And you heard "Satchmo"!'

'I did,' I said. 'It was swell. Ever been there?'

Madeleine shook her head. 'Too expensive. My friends and I go to the Howard Theatre.'

'You still dating that piano player?'

'Yeah, and it's still a secret, too. Momma would hang me out to dry with the rest of the laundry if she knew I was seeing a musician.'

'My lips are sealed.'

Sometimes I felt I was keeping enough secrets for my fellow boarders that they qualified for the 'L' file room at the OSS Registry.

I sharpened my pencil. I'd learned a couple of months ago that I had to do a rough draft of any letter I wrote to Joe on cheap paper, otherwise I'd be wasting good stationery. 'Dear Joe,' I began. Sweet heaven, what a weak way to begin a love letter! 'Dearest Joe'. No. Who was I trying to fool? Go ahead and write it down, coward. 'Darling'. That wasn't so hard, was it?

'Darling, I miss you terribly too. And I promise, promise faithfully, that I am coming to visit you just as soon as I can get away. It might be a last-minute decision because of work. That wouldn't be a problem, would it? If I sent you a telegram on a Friday afternoon saying I was just that minute catching a train?

'Your apartment sounds lovely. And it must be nice to live alone, at least for a little while. To be able to sleep, eat and read whenever you like sounds like heaven!

'Have you heard from Phoebe yet? Milt Junior has returned home. He's lost his left arm and will be living here for good. He was kind enough to move in with Henry so that Ada and I wouldn't lose our rooms. So when you come back to the District you'll need to find a new place to live. Do you know when that might be? When you might come home, that is?

'Miss you.' No! I missed my cat back home. Joe was my sweetheart. 'Darling, I can't wait to see you. Since you left my life has gone from Technicolor to grey.' So, so cheesy! But it would have to do. 'Love, Louise.' Not 'Love always.' Nothing was sure in life, especially during wartime.

I copied my draft on to the new stationery I'd bought at Woodies. It was cream with my initials engraved on it in sky blue. I'd never dreamed that someday I'd own monogrammed letter paper.

The large reception room on the first floor of the main OSS building was jammed with OSS staffers paying their respects to Paul Hughes. Since Hughes' remains had been shipped to Fredericksburg, his home, for his funeral, this small reception was his only memorial in the District. His co-workers had brought in vases of spring flowers for the tables, there was a picture of him on a table at the entrance to the room, and more friends had brought punch and cookies made with honey and molasses. He must have been popular.

I was at the reception out of morbid curiosity. I barely knew the man. But I still wondered about his death and I wanted to observe the people who attended his funeral, like the detectives in Agatha Christie's novels. Not that I had any evidence that Hughes' outlandish death was anything except bad luck. But I was obsessing over 'G'. Would 'G' be here? Was 'G' an actual initial, or some kind of shorthand? I mean, 'G' could be his barber! And last of all, was Paul meeting 'G' in Fredericksburg or in the District?

The most senior men in the room were Don Murray, my ex-boss and now Hughes' boss, and Major Wicker. When Wicker spotted me he shot me a look that ordered me in no uncertain terms not to speak to him. I wasn't insulted. He didn't want anyone to know we were acquainted.

After the guests mingled for a bit Don stood on a chair and began to speak about Hughes. How well liked he was, how hard-working, and how he would be missed. His final words were cut off by a strangled sob. Lots of the girls were dabbing at their eyes, but this was loud sobbing. I turned and saw Peggy Benton crying with a handkerchief pressed to her face. Her husband, Spencer, had a grip on her elbow. He looked quite embarrassed, even angry. I moved toward her to comfort her.

'Hush, be quiet,' Benton said to his wife, 'You're making a spectacle of yourself.'

'Paul was a very good friend,' Peggy answered him. 'It's all so sad!'

She buried her face in her handkerchief and sobbed again.

Benton turned to me. 'Mrs Pearlie, would you take Peggy outside, please, until she gets control of herself?' he said. 'I can't stand her bawling.'

'Certainly,' I said, taking Peggy's hand and leading her outside on to a narrow covered veranda. We perched on a bench. A wisteria vine that twisted around a marble column dangled its blossoms over our head.

'I know I embarrass Spencer,' Peggy said, breathing in short gulps, and rubbing her arm where her husband had gripped it. 'I'm always so emotional.'

'It's OK,' I said. 'If you can't cry over a friend's death, what can you cry about?'

'Spencer thinks I should restrain myself in public. It reflects on him, you see.'

I didn't comment on that.

'I didn't know you and Paul Hughes were so close,' I said.

'We were good friends. He came to Rose and Sadie's apartment several times. He didn't think that it was stupid for women to talk about serious subjects. Clark's the same way.'

Peggy's handkerchief was a sopping mess. I pulled out my own. 'Let me go dampen this,' I said. Inside I soaked the handkerchief in a water fountain, but not before I saw Don Murray and Major Wicker go into an office off the hall. Alone.

Peggy wiped her face with my handkerchief, then applied lipstick and powder.

'I hope I'm presentable enough to assume my role as Spencer's wife,' she said. 'Shall we go back inside?'

More people crowded the reception room, taking time off from lunch to pay their respects. I saw Rose talking to Clark and joined them while Peggy, pale but composed, went to her husband. Both Rose and Clark looked grim.

'Peggy is terribly upset,' I said to them. 'I had to take her outside.'

'She's very emotional,' Rose said. 'Cries over everything. Not that Paul's death isn't sad. And such a freak accident!'

'Sounds like he tried to come back to the District before he'd fully recovered,' Clark said.

'I'm surprised he tried to walk to the streetcar stop,' I said. 'You'd think he'd have caught a taxi home if he didn't feel well.'

Clark shrugged.

'If he had a fever he might not have been thinking clearly,' Rose said. She looked at her watch. 'I need to get back to work,' she said. We all did.

The reception room emptied quickly and I joined the crowd of people crossing 23rd Street to our building.

Just as I took the first step up the steep stone staircase to the renovated apartment house that housed the Research and Analysis Division a man touched my shoulder from behind.

'Ma'am,' he said, 'can you wait for a minute, please? I must speak to you.'

Startled, I pulled away. 'I don't know you,' I said. 'What do you want?'

He pulled out a small leather case and flipped it open, displaying a Metropolitan Police badge.

'Let's get away from this crowd,' he said, nodding down the hill to a spot where a bunch of forsythia bushes clustered, blooming bright yellow.

'I need to get back to work,' I said.

'This won't take a minute. I insist.'

I glanced around. None of my co-workers, scurrying back to their offices, noticed us.

The two of us sheltered behind the thicket of forsythia bushes. I had a powerful sense of foreboding. What did this policeman want with me?

'I'm Detective Sergeant Royal, Metropolitan Police,' he said to me, showing me his badge again so I could see the number clearly. 'Write it down if you like, check me out.'

He was an older man, plenty old enough to be retired. He probably still worked because of the war. He was dressed in a well worn but respectable suit and tie. A dilapidated fedora, which looked like it had repelled a lot of rain in its time, covered grizzled hair. Deep frown lines scoured his face between his eyebrows. Royal leaned heavily on one leg as if the other one hurt him.

'You are Mrs Louise Pearlie,' he said.

'How did you know that?' I asked. He knew my name and had intercepted me walking up the steps to an OSS divisional office. Again I had a sense of apprehension. I was wary that a stranger, even a policeman, knew my name and where I worked.

'I'm the detective who was called to the scene of Paul Hughes' drowning,' he said. 'Last Monday. And you're the woman who visited his landlady, Mrs Nighy, the following Wednesday, to question her about Hughes' absence from work, long before the Metropolitan Police even knew who the man was. I want to talk to you about that visit.'

Oh my God! I had given Mrs Nighy my real name! And identified myself as coming from Hughes' office! What had I been thinking! That was a beginner's mistake. No matter how casual I thought the inquiry was, I should never have given anyone a way to trace me back to OSS!

'How did you find out where I worked?' I asked.

'An FBI agent owed me a favor,' he said. The FBI kept secured files on all government personnel. Mine was a little thicker than most. 'Oh, and I know Paul Hughes worked here too.'

I feigned innocence as best I could.

'Of course, Detective, I would be glad to help, but I don't see why you need to talk to me. Poor Mr Hughes drowned accidentally. At work we couldn't have known that, we only wanted to know where he was. I'm just a file clerk. My boss sent me to his boarding house to ask about him.'

'Did he?' Royal asked. 'Did Hughes drown accidentally? Are you sure of that?'

Stragglers from the reception came hurrying up the hill, glancing at me curiously as they went by. I had to get away from Royal before he attracted any more attention to me.

'I don't think my superiors would want me to talk to you,' I said. 'I'd have to ask permission.'

'Ma'am,' he said, 'if you don't meet me for breakfast at seven a.m. tomorrow at the café on the corner of Twenty-first and "H", I'm going to get in my police car and drive right here. Then I'm going to limp right up those stairs and tell your boss I need to speak to you and I'm going to be cranky because those steep stone steps are going to make my knee ache. And at the end of all this your boss will learn that you made a mistake that is going to damage his good opinion of you.'

I couldn't take the chance that Major Wicker would find out I had done something so stupid as to give Mrs Nighy my real name. I'd be doing nothing but filing index cards until the war was over and then be grateful to find work as a shop girl.

'All right,' I said, 'I'll be there.'

'Smart girl,' he said. 'Don't be late.'

'I'll have two eggs over medium, bacon, and biscuits with butter and jelly, and plenty of coffee,' Royal said.

'Adam and Eve on a raft,' the waitress repeated. 'But we ain't got no jelly.'

Royal showed her his badge, and she shrugged. 'OK. Maybe we got a little jelly. Ma'am?' she asked me. 'Are you ready to order?'

'Toast and tea,' I said. The waitress ripped the order off her pad and took it behind the kitchen counter where she clipped it to the rotating order rack.

'Off your feed?' Royal asked.

'I didn't sleep very well last night,' I said. I hadn't been able to eat anything except crackers since Royal introduced himself to me yesterday. I was so fearful that my bosses at OSS would discover that I was too careless to be trusted with my Top Secret clearance.

It was early and the café wasn't as crowded as it would be in half an hour. Royal pulled a chair over from an empty table and propped a leg up on it.

'Bad knee,' he said. 'Second Battle of the Marne. It was a miracle I didn't lose the leg. Sometimes I wish I had.'

'Detective,' I said. 'What is it you want to ask me? I'm happy to cooperate. But I have to be at work at eight thirty.'

The waitress brought our food. Royal tucked into his and I nibbled at my toast.

'Mrs Pearlie,' he said, 'I want you to help me find out who murdered Paul Hughes.'

'What!' I said. 'What do you mean?' I felt like the tiny bit of toast I'd swallowed was choking me. 'Hughes drowned.'

'That he did,' Royal said. 'But not until someone knocked him unconscious and tossed him into the Tidal Basin.'

'I thought he fainted and hit his head . . .'

'If Mr Hughes had fainted near enough to the Tidal Basin to land on the rocks he'd be covered with bruises, not just the honking great goose egg he had on his head. I think he was struck from behind with one of those rocks and dumped unconscious into the water.'

Royal paused to butter his biscuit.

'But the case has been closed,' I said.

'Ma'am,' Royal said, 'what I am telling you is that the minute your friend Mr Hughes was identified word came down from above to close the file on his death. Which means I am forbidden to investigate his death further. Officially Hughes died from an accidental drowning despite all the signs that his death was a homicide.'

'You don't know he didn't just drown!' I argued. 'Everyone has accepted it.'

Hughes leaned toward me and lowered his voice. 'I'm an old policeman,' he said. 'I've seen everything. When a dead man has nothing in his pockets, no wallet, no pocketknife, no handkerchief, not even a canceled bus ticket, he's been stripped for a reason. What, you think a turtle made off with his wallet? The man was murdered, that's all there is to it, and your Oh So Secret friends are hushing it up!'

I was too shaken to speak.

'And the District Chief of Detectives is too gutless to defy them,' Royal said, the blood vessels at his temples bulging. 'And I'm forbidden to investigate a homicide. I'm expected to ignore cold-blooded murder and occupy myself with stolen ration coupons! You know what else? My lieutenant, who can barely shave, thinks I'm too decrepit to do good work anymore! The only reason I was dispatched to the Hughes scene was

because it was supposedly just an accident.' Royal kept his
voice to a whisper, but his fists were clenched so that his knuckles
were white. I hoped he didn't have a heart attack.

'If the police did classify Hughes' death as murder,' Royal
continued, 'I'd be pulled off the case pronto and some hotshot
young fellow who'd been to the new police academy would
get the job.'

I kept my mouth shut. This guy harbored a grudge that
predated Hughes' death and I had no intention of commenting
on it.

'Sorry,' Royal said. 'I get worked up sometimes. Want some
jelly for your toast?' He pushed the dish of strawberry jelly
over to me. The way I felt I couldn't eat it if my life depended
on it.

But what Royal had said about Hughes' death made sense.
I thought through it all while Royal finished his breakfast and
drank his coffee refill. After the waitress took away our plates,
mine looking like a mouse with a toothache had been nibbling
at the edges of my toast, I got down to business.

'What do you want from me?' I asked. 'I'm just a file clerk.'

'A file clerk who was trusted by an armchair general from
your three-letter agency to question Mrs Nighy about Hughes'
absence. Mrs Nighy happily told me your name when I called
on her after we found out the results of Hughes' fingerprints.
But when I got back to the precinct my lieutenant told me
that the case was closed – the coroner had ruled accidental
death. I was supposed to go home and take a nap or something.
But I had your name. So I tracked you down and found you
at your Oh So Social government agency run by college boys.
And you know what? I am going to solve this murder if it's
the last thing I do, and throw it in the Chief of Detectives'
face! And you're going to help me.'

If OSS had insisted the District police close the investigation on Paul Hughes' death it meant one of two things. First,
they accepted Hughes' death as accidental and just wanted to
keep the story out of the news. Spy agencies liked their privacy.
Or, OSS was suspicious, too, and wanted to investigate Hughes'

possible murder themselves, for the same reason, to keep it out of the public eye.

'Tell me everything you learned at Mrs Nighy's house on Wednesday, and I'll keep you out of all this.'

I didn't hesitate. I didn't see that I knew much of any importance, not enough to imperil my career. So I told him. How Mrs Nighy didn't have a telephone. How she got a telegram from Hughes' mother telling her that he was ill and wouldn't be back until he was well.

'Anything else?'

'That's all.'

'Baloney. I don't believe it. Hughes' room is right in the front of the house. Didn't you go in it? You're a spy, for God's sake.'

'Keep your voice down, and I'm not. OK, I searched Hughes' room.'

'Tell me about it.'

So I told him that Hughes' personal effects were still in his bedroom and that Mrs Nighy told me he never took luggage to his mother's because he kept a set of clothes and toiletries at her place.

'Anything else at all that was suspicious?'

'Not that I can think of.' There was no way I was going to tell Royal about 'G'. I was willing to share all the throwaway information I could to save my job, but not something that might actually be valuable to OSS. I had given Hughes' note directly into the hands of Major Wicker of the OSS Security Office, and I wasn't going to say anything to Royal about it, even if he held my feet over a fire.

The café began to fill with government workers in a hurry. Hughes handed three dollars to our waitress and told her to keep the change. He lifted his leg carefully off the chair he'd commandeered, which he shoved back to its spot at a nearby table.

'I have to go,' I said. Thank God this was over. I'd told the man all I knew and would soon be shot of him.

'One more thing,' he said.

'I've told you everything I know. I'm done.'

'I need you to locate Paul Hughes' personnel file for me.'

'No!' I said. 'Are you a lunatic?'

'No ma'am,' he said. 'Stubborn and cranky, but not loony. Find Hughes' personnel file and take notes on it. You can leave out the secret bits. I want to know the basics – birth, residence, education, parents' address, all that everyday stuff. If I was assigned to the case I could find it out myself.'

'I can't!'

'Sure you can. Unless you want me to stroll over to that big building with the columns – the one that used to be the naval hospital – and tell them how I found you. Or get in touch with the FBI. They're familiar with you, aren't they?'

'That's blackmail!'

'Sure it is. You don't doubt I'd do it, do you?'

'No, you creep!'

'Don't hold yourself back.'

'You bastard!' I think that was the first time I'd ever spoken that curse out loud.

'I have no intention of harming you, Mrs Pearlie, but I've had a young man murdered in my jurisdiction. I intend to find out who did it. If some important government agency then decides it has to be hushed up, well, so be it. But we're going to know who the murderer is. Otherwise we can't pretend to be more civilized than the scum we're fighting.'

He drained his cup of coffee. 'I'll meet you here tomorrow, same time,' he said. 'And you can give me your notes on Hughes' file. OK?'

'No,' I said.

'What?' he said.

'This is how it will be. I won't remove any documents from OSS. I won't photocopy any documents. I won't take any notes. I'll memorize the basics about Hughes, information you might be able to find out for yourself if you hadn't been taken off the case.'

'All I want is his birth date, his mother's name and address in Fredericksburg, stuff like that. Something to start with.'

'That's all you're getting.'

'Fine. I'll meet you here tomorrow.'

'No. Wait in front of the Western Market on 'K', just past 23rd. I'll meet you there. We'll walk to a café of my choice for breakfast.'

Royal leaned into me and whispered, smiling, 'You *are* a spy.'

I whispered back. 'This is not a joking matter. Use that word again and I'll go straight to OSS Security and tell them all about you. I'm sure blackmailing a government employee, especially in time of war, is a seditious act.'

FIVE

Give the female employee [. . .] a definite day-long
schedule of duties so that she'll keep busy without bothering the management for instructions every few minutes.
Numerous properties say that women make excellent
workers when they have their jobs cut out for them but
that they lack initiative in finding work themselves.
'1943 Guide to Hiring Women', *Mass Transportation*
magazine, July 1943.

I stayed at my desk as lunch hour neared waiting for the number
of people in the Registry to dwindle. I wanted as few witnesses
to my search for Paul Hughes' personnel file as possible. By
twelve thirty the Registry was as empty as it ever got.

I made my way to the personnel index files and looked up
Paul Hughes' card. Good, the 'H' personnel files were located
just one floor up outside a ladies' restroom, which could serve
as my cover.

There was just one other girl in the toilet and she ignored
me, focusing on putting on her make-up and brushing her hair.
I didn't recognize her, so there was a good chance that she
didn't know me either. I washed my face and hands and cleaned
my glasses, waiting for her to leave. When I left the restroom
I found the hall empty, so I darted down the 'H' aisle, opened
the correct file drawer and riffled through the contents. Hughes'
file wasn't there. In its place was a yellow card that read
'moved to L file'.

Hughes' personnel records had been sent to the Limited
file, which was only available to authorized personnel. It was
created to house the Special Intelligence Branch documents,
but the big men at OSS could stamp any file they wanted with
the 'L' designation.

Who would send Hughes' personnel file to the Limited file room? Perhaps Major Wicker or Don Murray wanted to keep Hughes' personal information away from prying staff. Like me! I slid the file cabinet door closed and made my way back to my own desk. Lunchtime was over. The returning file clerks were clustered around the coffee cart that was parked in the middle of the Registry aisles. I got my cup and joined a few of the girls standing around the cart. I was glad to see Ruth, who'd worked with me in the early days. She was a Mount Holyoke graduate who wore pearls every day, even under a denim jumpsuit.

'I haven't seen you on the bus recently,' I said. 'Have you been coming in early?'

She shook her head. 'Jack picks me up almost every morning now,' she said. 'I didn't know when we started dating how convenient it would be to have a beau with a motorcycle and sidecar.'

She drained her cup and grasped the handle of her file cart. That's what Ruth did. She filed all day long, pushing her cart down long aisles, A to Z, until her cart was empty, then filling it up again at the return tables in the Reading Room. She wore gloves to protect her hands and a leather apron to cover her clothes.

'Want to have lunch today?' I asked.

'Can't,' she answered, 'I'm meeting Jack. I made a picnic lunch. We like to eat outdoors when it's pretty.'

She expertly maneuvered her cart in the narrow aisle and headed toward the elevator.

I went back to my desk with my cup of coffee and mulled over Hughes' personnel file.

I had Top Secret clearance so I could go into the Limited file room. There was an 'L' return table just outside the door to said file room, and the guard knew who was authorized to pick up those files and take them inside. I just had to wait until there were files stacked on the table that needed to be returned, collect them, take them inside to put away and locate Hughes' file. Simple.

I walked over to the Reading Room. Almost every chair was full already. The Trident Conference was in full swing and the Joint Chiefs needed answers to dozens of questions. The 'L' return table was empty. I'd need to wait until it was stacked with files to pull off my plan.

On my next trip to the Reading Room the return table held enough files for me to look like I was working when I picked up an armful. The guard at the door to the 'L' room recognized me but he did his duty and checked my tag – which displayed my picture, employee number and security clearance, but not my name – and nodded for me to go inside.

Once inside the dim room I breathed a heavy sigh of relief. I turned on the bank of overhead lights. The only window let in little light, but that was compromised by the heavy bars that criss-crossed it, and drawn blinds. A notice read 'Do Not Open the Blinds or Window'. I felt almost as if I were in jail.

I quickly filed the folders I had picked up from the return table. I paused in front of the 'H' drawer, suddenly nervous. I could sense my heart pounding and feel the sweat gathering in the small of my back. I had to do this, I told myself. I couldn't take the chance that Sergeant Royal would tell OSS that I'd made such a basic mistake when questioning Mrs Nighy. Besides, I had the clearance to be here and I wasn't going to reveal any secrets. It would be OK.

I found Paul Hughes' personnel file. 'Analyst, Europe/Africa Section', stamped 'L' and 'Top Secret'. Why Top Secret? Swiftly I opened it. And my hope for a quick exit from this messy business vanished.

Paul Hughes' parents were both dead. His father, Samuel Paul Hughes, had died in 1937. His mother, Mariella Hodgson Hughes, died the following year. Hughes' next of kin was a sister, Mary Hughes Perkins, who lived in Knoxville, Tennessee. A mortuary receipt showed that Hughes' body had been shipped to a funeral home in Knoxville.

Hughes' home address was listed as the boarding house where he lived. His death certificate was signed by a District medical examiner that listed the cause of death as 'drowning

incidental to head injury'. I flipped through the autopsy
pictures. Years of cleaning fish had given me a strong
stomach. The photo of Hughes' head showed a very substan-
tial bruise behind his right ear. He would have had to fall
from a great height to have had a lump like that. And if
he had, why weren't there more bruises on his body, as
Royal had suggested?

If that wasn't enough startling information, the letters and
numbers on the Western Union telegram from Hughes'
'mother' to Mrs Nighy had been deciphered. It had been sent
from a Western Union office located a very short walk from
the Tidal Basin.

I looked up from the file and took a deep breath. Dust motes
floated in the strips of light that found their way through the
window blinds. Fortunately I was still alone. If someone had
been with me in the room I'm sure they would have noticed my
reaction to the unexpected information in Hughes' file.

Next I read Hughes' job application to OSS. He'd earned
a Masters degree in economics from Yale. OSS was packed
with Yalies. General Donovan himself had gone to Yale. He
recruited his staff from his cronies and old professors and their
protégés. And most Yale graduates spoke a second language,
unlike graduates from many other American universities.

Hughes listed four references. Two were clearly professors.
The other two were Spencer Benton and Clark Leach. This
surprised me at first. But it made sense. If Clark and Hughes
knew each other at Yale, and had similar political ideas, then
of course they might continue to meet socially once they were
in OSS. This helped explain why Leach, despite his lofty rank
at OSS, hobnobbed with Rose's group. His friend Paul Hughes
was already a member.

Nowhere in the few papers in Hughes' file was a name I
could identify as 'G'.

I replaced Hughes' file in the cabinet and went back to my
desk. Now I knew why someone had stamped 'L' and 'Top
Secret' on Hughes' file. It contained explosive information.
That Hughes didn't visit his mother in Fredericksburg on the

weekends. That Spencer Benton and Clark Leach knew Hughes
at Yale. That the telegram to Mrs Nighy was sent from a
Western Union office near the Tidal Basin. At lunch I took a very long walk. I bought a hot dog from
a cart on the street. I couldn't finish it and tossed it to a skinny
dog begging scraps from the other government girls eating
their lunches on blankets in the grass. I walked for blocks. By
the time I got back to work I had managed to minimize the
significance of the facts I'd found. I figured that Hughes' file
had been sequestered just to keep curious staff members from
looking at it. As for the so-called visits to his mother in
Fredericksburg, maybe Hughes had a girlfriend he spent weekends with and didn't want anyone to know about. Yes, that
made sense. The girlfriend could have sent the telegram to
Mrs Nighy, omitting her return address from the message. And
if Hughes had the flu and decided to go back to his boarding
house anyway, why couldn't he have fainted and hit a damn
big rock on the edge of the Tidal Basin before he fell into it
and drowned? As for his empty pockets, I was stumped. But
then I thought of an explanation for that too. Perhaps he was
wearing a light jacket and took it off when he began to feel
faint. Then it could have been stolen, along with his wallet.

But what about 'G'?

Oh, for God's sake! Just this minute I didn't give a damn.
I intended to give Royal all the information he asked for
tomorrow morning and extricate myself from this mess!

Ada held one end of the measuring tape at the corner of Phoebe's
davenport while I read the tape at the other end. 'Sixty-two
inches,' I said, scribbling the measurement into a notebook.

Phoebe was out of the house at a bridge party, so Ada and
I were taking the opportunity to estimate how much fabric we'd
need to slipcover Phoebe's lounge set for her. The davenport
and two matching club chairs were so worn in places the muslin
backing showed through the upholstery.

'OK,' Ada said. 'Now we need to do the back.'

She leaned over the back cushions and dangled the tape

measure over the back of the davenport. I crept under the console table behind the davenport to read the tape.

'It doesn't need to be perfect,' Ada said, 'just close enough to know how much fabric we need to buy.'

'Where did your friend say this discount fabric store is?' I asked.

'Just outside the District in Chevy Chase,' Ada said. 'We'll have to borrow Phoebe's car to get there – and to get back with yards of fabric. We'll need a good excuse.'

'We'll think of something,' I said.

'I hope she likes what we pick out,' Ada said.

'If it's floral and has some pink in it she'll love it.'

The telephone in the hall rang and Dellaphine picked it up.

'Yes ma'am,' Dellaphine said into the receiver, 'she's in. But her social calendar is mighty full.'

I dropped the chair cushion I was measuring and ran out into the hall, pulling the telephone out of Dellaphine's hand.

'You're a barrel of laughs,' I said to Dellaphine.

'I just says it like I sees it,' she said, a wide smile splitting her usually solemn face.

'Hello?' I said into the receiver.

'It's me,' Rose said. 'I was wondering if you'd like to do something with me and Sadie tonight. We're bored. We're thinking of going to the movies.'

'I would, but I'm in the middle of something,' I said, glancing into the lounge, where Ada was writing figures in the notebook. She looked up at me.

'You go on,' Ada said. 'I can finish this.'

'You sure?'

'Yes, I'm sure,' Ada said. 'Go have a good time.'

'I can come,' I said to Rose. 'What's the plan?'

'We want to see *Above Suspicion* over at the Capitol Theatre. With Fred MacMurray and Joan Crawford. Have you heard of it?'

'Sure,' I said. 'I've read the book.'

'If we meet at Thompsons Cafeteria in half an hour we'll have time to get dessert or something first.'

'OK,' I said, glancing at my wristwatch. 'I'll see you there.'

Thompsons Cafeteria had about two dozen tables ranged down the middle of the restaurant between the buffet line and the short-order counter. Though it was still early in the evening, the dinner rush was over and the restaurant was half empty. Sadie hadn't eaten dinner yet so we got in the buffet queue. Sadie piled her plate full of meatloaf, mashed potatoes, green beans and corn. Rose and I pounced on the last two pieces of peach pie.

We found a table at the front of the restaurant so, as Sadie observed, we could watch interesting people pass by the front window. 'Maybe we'll spot some hunky soldiers,' Sadie said.

'They're all children,' Rose said.

'Not the officers,' Sadie said. She peered at the meatloaf on her fork. 'I think this is mostly breadcrumbs,' she said. She popped the piece into her mouth. 'Oh, well, it tastes good.'

'I guess Peggy couldn't come?' I asked.

'No,' Sadie said. 'She's cooking dinner for Spencer and maybe darning his socks.'

'I'm never getting married,' Rose said.

'So you've said,' Sadie said. 'But you can date, can't you? And not all husbands are like Spencer Benton.'

'What about you, Louise?' Rose said. 'Do you think you'll ever get married?'

'Well, I've been married,' I answered, scraping up the tiny crumbs of my peach pie. I would swear there was real sugar in it. 'My husband died of pneumonia six years ago.'

'You dope,' Sadie said to Rose. 'Didn't you notice there's a "Mrs" before her name?'

Rose laid her head on the table and crossed her arms over it. 'I am so terribly sorry,' she said, her voice muffled. 'This must be my stupid day. Please forgive me.'

'What was your husband like?' Sadie persisted. 'Did you like being married?'

'Do you think you could repress your curiosity for a few

seconds until I can see if Louise is mad at me?' Rose asked, sitting back up.

'I'm not mad at you at all; it's been six years since Bill died,' I said to her. 'And yes, Sadie, I did like being married. Bill was my childhood sweetheart. He had a good job, and during the Depression only one person in a family could work. I had fun fixing up our apartment and learning to cook. We went out to the movies or to a fish fry at church on the weekends. I didn't know there was anything else.'

'I'm so sorry,' Rose said again.

'For heaven's sake,' I said. 'Forget about it.'

'Do you want to get married again?' Sadie asked.

'If I meet the right man, sure,' I said. I thought about Joe. I was in love with him, but he was not the right man! I wasn't even sure the name he was using was his real name. 'But I don't want to get married just for marriage's sake. I really like working and supporting myself.' By which I meant that I was thrilled not being dependent on my parents, not cleaning slimy fish at their fish camp, not feeling like every eye at my Baptist church was trained on me and not being introduced to every halfway presentable bachelor in Wilmington, North Carolina. Especially the elderly widowers who chewed tobacco.

I was finishing my coffee when a sudden silence fell over the restaurant. It was so palpable that our awareness of it interrupted our conversation. The eyes of everyone in the place were fixed on the door. Three black girls had entered the cafeteria and gotten into line at the buffet. The colored man serving at the first station stared at them, his eyes wide open and his spatula hovering over the meatloaf. I saw him swallow hard, his Adam's apple bobbing, looking at the girls, then over at the white manager at the cash register. He was afraid of what might happen next. The manager, a thin bald man with a dishtowel tucked into his apron pocket, came around the front of the buffet line and strode toward the girls.

Every pair of eyes in the restaurant fixed on the unfolding drama.

'What do you girls think you are doing here?' the manager

said, his chin jutting out. He gripped the rails of the buffet line with his right hand as if he might rip a piece of the metal out and shake it at them.

'We're getting our dinner,' the first girl in line said. She was older than the other two girls and looked almost masculine in black trousers, with short curly hair and no make-up.

The diners stirred then, murmuring and clattering their silverware. I looked around me. I was relieved to see that most of the people in the dining room didn't seem hostile to the black girls. They seemed to be waiting mostly, to see what the manager would do and what would happen next. There were a few tables, though, where the restaurant patrons were quite upset. I could tell by their ugly expressions.

Sadie gripped my arm and then Rose's. 'Oh my God,' she whispered. 'It's a sit-in!'

'A what?' I said.

'The girls must be Howard University students,' Rose said. 'There's a campus group that organizes what they call sit-ins. They go into restaurants and try to get served.'

I'd protest too if I were those girls. In all of the downtown District there were only two places where a Negro could get a meal and use the restroom: the YWCA cafeteria on 11th and 'K', and Union Station.

'Sadie, let go of me, you're breaking my wrist,' Rose said.

'This is so exciting!' Sadie said, bouncing a little in her seat. 'What do you think is going to happen?'

'You girls need to leave,' the manager said again. 'We don't serve coloreds.'

'Why not?' said one of the girls, smart in a hot pink and yellow sundress with dangling pink earrings to match. 'Our money's as good as anyone else's.'

'Now you all know you can get just as good a meal up at the Y,' the manager said.

'It's too far away. We're on our way to the movies,' said a third girl, who wore her hair in a mane curl tied back at the base of her neck, the first one I'd seen outside a fashion magazine. She'd pulled all her hair back, tied it at the base of her neck with a thick ribbon, then tucked the rest of her hair under the ribbon. I liked it.

'It's against the law,' the manager said. 'You know that.'

The manager glanced over at the front door to the restaurant, where some people had stopped at the door, noticed the scene and turned away. A few remained, their faces pressed to the plate-glass window, voyeurs eager to see what was going to happen. Most of the diners inside began to collect their belongings and head for the exit, leaving uneaten food on their plates. A few of them shot nasty looks at the girls on their way out.

Please God, I thought, no violence. No beatings. I had seen a grocer back home beat his colored boy for spilling flour on the floor of his store and I'd never forgotten it.

The older girl, the one wearing trousers, reached out her hand to shake hands with the manager. He looked at her in pure astonishment and refused her outstretched hand.

'I'm Pauli Murray,' she said, introducing herself anyway. 'I'm a law student at Howard University. There are no segregation laws in the District. And you haven't got a sign in your window saying you don't serve Negroes.'

I saw smiles cross the faces of the colored man who served the meatloaf and the white-haired colored lady further down the buffet who dished up the vegetables.

By now most of the diners had slipped out the door. A few tables remained. One with two older couples who just kept eating. Some young servicemen leaned back in their chairs, watching as if they were at a baseball game. I was concerned about a group of three men wearing Capital Transit uniforms at a table in the center of the big dining room. They were shifting in their seats and putting out their cigarettes as if they were about to do something.

'We have to stay,' Rose said to Sadie and me. 'And help them.'

I thought we should do our best to convince the colored girls to leave the cafeteria with us, but then I decided instead that we should stand our ground, no matter what happened. I doubted the protesters would leave anyway.

'What should we do?' I asked.

Sadie slid out of her chair.

'I'm going to join those girls,' she said. 'I wish I could get hold of my reporter friend.'

'Louise and I are coming with you,' Rose said.

'No,' Sadie said, 'you two work for the government. Best stay out of it. Mr Layman doesn't care what messes I get into.'

Sadie marched right up to the girls, grabbed a plate and joined them in the queue.

'What are you doing?' the manager asked her. 'Stay out of this!'

'Getting some dessert to eat with my friends here,' Sadie said.

'Look,' he said to her, 'what are you, a pinko? We don't serve coloreds here. That's just the way it is, you know that. I'll lose all my customers if these girls don't leave right now.'

The crowd outside had grown, lining the front windows of the restaurant.

Then the police arrived.

'I didn't know the District had any colored policemen,' Rose said.

'I'll bet these are all of them,' I said.

The Negro lieutenant left two of the three colored patrolmen on guard outside and brought the third into the restaurant with him. He looked utterly careworn, his skin more grey than black.

'All right,' he said, 'what's going on here?'

'These girls won't leave,' the manager answered. 'This one here,' he said, nodding at Pauli Murray, 'says there ain't no laws against them eating here. That's not true, right?'

'No, they're right,' said the police lieutenant, whose nametag identified him as E. Mosely. 'But,' he said, glaring with disapproval at the girls, 'it's accepted, and you girls know that. Move along now and get your supper at the Y.'

'There's no sign in the window saying colored people can't eat here,' Sadie piped up, waving her plate toward the buffet line for emphasis. 'How were they supposed to know? They should be able to get their dinner here like everyone else.'

Pauli Murray moved further along the buffet line with her plate. 'I'll have the catfish, please,' she said. The colored man behind the steam table lifted up a spatula piled high with fried fish.

The manager, with his eyes on the gathering crowd outside, stood between the girl and the buffet. The Capital Transit men stood up, ready to intervene. The crowd outside murmured. The trouble they'd been hoping for had arrived.

The colored lieutenant stretched out his hands toward the manager, palms up. 'Looky here,' he said. 'Let's make a deal. You let these girls eat here this evening, tomorrow you post a sign in your window saying your place is segregated. How about that? Then all these folks can go home and no one gets hurt. You don't want your place in the newspapers, do you?'

The manager gave in. 'OK,' he said. 'Just this once. The dinner hour is almost over anyway. You girls go on down the line, but don't ever come back here.'

The men in the Capital Transit uniforms moved toward the girls, but the Negro policemen stood between them. I'd had enough. I didn't care if they beat me up too, this was too awful to just sit and watch.

I jumped up from my chair and grabbed the arm of one of the Capital Transit drivers, the one who was clearly the leader. He pulled back from me in surprise. 'Stay out of this,' he said.

I glanced at my watch, pointedly. 'I believe your dinner hour is over,' I said. 'Aren't you due back at your streetcars at eight? Or do you want to get thrown in jail for starting a race riot? We've got plenty of witnesses here to testify who started it.'

He tried to stare me down, his fists clenching and unclenching. But then one of his friends took his arm. 'Come on, Clem, let's go. I don't want to get fired.'

'OK,' he said, then glared at Pauli Murray, who'd calmly progressed through the buffet line, adding French fries and butter beans to her fish. 'You there,' he said, 'you heard what the man said, don't ever come back here.' She ignored him.

The Negro policeman opened the door and the drivers left,

along with the crowd outside that had been waiting for the excitement to start.

'Good work,' Rose said, as I sat back down at our table. I'd gotten a coffee refill, figuring we needed to stay to see the colored girls leave safely. I wished it was a Martini.

'I think we're going to miss the movie,' I said.

'Better to watch history being made,' Rose said.

'You think this was that important?'

'Yes I do. Social movements don't ever stop. They can be delayed, but in the end things move on.'

I shook my head. 'I don't believe this country will ever be integrated,' I said.

'No one thought a bunch of Russian peasants could overthrow the czar, either,' Rose said.

Sadie had eaten her jello with the colored girls, but came back to our table when they left the restaurant, smiling broadly. The policemen, who'd been guarding the door all this time, left with them. Sadie was still wound up.

'Pauli said the Howard students are going to integrate the District and no one can stop them!' she told us.

The manager flipped the sign on the door to 'Closed'. 'Time for you girls to leave,' he said. As we went out the door he said, 'And don't you ever come back here either.'

When I got back to 'Two Trees' I was exhausted. I had pain between my shoulder blades from the tension that had built up in me in the restaurant. Propped up on my pillows I sipped a Martini. It was smart of those Howard students to send girls to the restaurants. If they'd been boys, I didn't doubt there'd have been an awful fight.

Royal was waiting outside the Western Market for me, leaning up against the big plate-glass storefront to take the weight off his game leg, smoking a cigarette. When he saw me he dropped the butt on the sidewalk and ground it into the cement with the tip of his shoe.

'Where to?' Royal asked.

'Across the street,' I said.

We slid on to the cracked seats in one of the six booths in the tiny café. A fan missing one blade slowly turned overhead. 'It looks dingy, but it's clean,' I said. 'Great biscuits.' My stomach was still somewhat dicey so biscuits would be all I could eat.

The young colored waiter came out from behind the counter to wait on us.

'Coffee,' Royal said. 'Adam and Eve on a raft over medium, and my friend here tells me the biscuits here are good.'

'They're the best in town. From my grandma's recipe.'

'I'll just have biscuits and milk,' I said. 'Do you have real butter? Jelly?'

'We got butter,' he said. 'But no jelly. How about some honey? We bring it up from my cousin's farm in Virginia.'

'Yes, please,' I said.

When Royal's coffee came he pulled an aspirin bottle out of his coat pocket and tossed down two with his first gulp.

'I hope your leg really hurts,' I said.

He grinned at me. 'Yes ma'am,' he said. 'It does. Bourbon kills the pain best, but it's a bit early in the day for that.'

The colored boy brought our food.

'These biscuits are real good,' Royal said.

I mixed up butter and honey into one thick spread and layered it on a biscuit. It went down well between gulps of milk so I ate another one.

When we were done the waiter cleared our plates and Royal had another full cup of coffee. Then he pulled out his narrow pad and pencil.

I considered very carefully what information I would share with him.

'Paul Hughes' parents are dead,' I said. 'There is no mother in Fredericksburg.'

Royal glanced up from his notes, his eyebrows raised.

'No kidding!' he said.

'His next of kin is listed as a sister in Knoxville. That's where his body was shipped.'

'I'll be damned.'

I told Royal a few more selected facts such as Hughes' birth date and his education at Yale, and then delivered the bombshell. 'The telegram, the one that was supposed to come from Hughes' mother: it was sent from the Western Union office 434 Twelfth, Southwest.'

'Wow,' he said, 'so close to the Tidal Basin!'

'I know. What do you think it means?'

'We don't have enough information to connect the dots yet, but it's a hell of a coincidence.'

I said nothing about Clark Leach and Spencer Benton or about Hughes' file being transferred to the 'L' room.

'That's all the information you have?' Royal asked.

I shrugged. 'That's it,' I said. 'The file could have been edited by someone in Personnel after Hughes' death, I suppose.'

'Must have been,' he said.

'Well,' I said, 'I can't say it was nice knowing you. Goodbye. I'm going to work now.'

But as I began to rise from my seat Royal reached across the table and grabbed my wrist, hard.

'You're not done yet, Mrs Pearlie. I have another job for you.'

I pulled back from his grip and he let me go. At this point there was nothing to keep me from just leaving the café. I was fairly sure he wouldn't report me to OSS now. But I couldn't repress my own curiosity. I lowered myself back down to the bench.

'What now?' I said.

'I want you to go to that Western Union office,' he said. 'Even if the return address wasn't printed on the telegram they'll have a record of it.'

I knew immediately that I would do it. I wanted to know myself.

'What if it's just a girlfriend's?' I said. 'Hughes could have spent his weekends with her, pretending to be visiting his mother. And when he fell ill the girlfriend sent the telegram to Mrs Nighy, leaving her return address off the telegram message.'

'Maybe,' he said. 'Maybe not. But I need to know if I'm going to find out who murdered Mr Hughes.'

I wasn't convinced Hughes was murdered myself. But I wanted to know who sent that telegram, too, and I figured that the only way I would know was if I checked it out for him. And I'd already done enough to get myself fired; what was one more infraction?

'OK,' I said. 'I'll go. But I can't until the weekend. I can't leave work without a very good excuse and I'm not going to lie.'

Royal nodded. 'Good. I'll catch up with you on Sunday afternoon. Where can we meet?'

'Around the corner and down the alley from the filling station across the street from my boarding house.'

'I'll be there.'

After Mrs Pearlie left the café Royal called for another cup of coffee and lit a cigarette. If that woman really was just a file clerk, he thought, she was wasted. She had only given him the very basic information from Hughes' file. She was keeping her mouth shut about everything else. But he had her hooked now. He could tell by the expression in her eyes when he asked her to go to that Western Union office for him. She wanted to know what had happened to Hughes as badly as he did.

Since Hughes' case had been closed Royal wasn't permitted to investigate. He couldn't make any official inquiries without his superiors finding out. Without Mrs Pearlie he'd be without resources. He just hoped he could keep her interested long enough to help him solve the case.

I couldn't figure out Clark Leach. He'd offered to pick me up and drive me over to Rose and Sadie's again. Leach was a big shot. He was a member of the inner circle at OSS, escorting China's representative Dr T.V. Soong at the Trident Conference. Why on earth was he bothering with me? And why did he want to spend his Thursday evenings at Rose's little salon to begin with? He stuck out like a sore thumb. He was the only man there. Of course, I reminded myself, Paul Hughes had been a member too, and from Hughes' file it looked like he and Leach must have known each other at Yale. I promised myself to find out tonight how well they'd known each other.

After he'd picked me up Leach and I stopped at the Western Market to buy supplies for the evening. We bought a six-pack of beer and potato chips. I'd already gone by the liquor store for a bottle of Gordon's gin.

'Peggy isn't coming,' Rose said, as she met the two of us at the door. She had already changed out of her work clothes into jeans rolled up at the ankle and a sweatshirt. Sadie wore a pair of smart lounging pajamas that I immediately coveted.

Sadie took our offerings into the kitchen while Rose plopped on the sofa. 'Sit,' she said to me, patting the sofa next to her. 'You look done in. Let Clark make our drinks.' She extended her empty glass and Clark obligingly went over to the make-shift bar, an old dresser topped with a painted tray crowded with liquor and a Martini shaker.

Sadie came in from the kitchen with the potato chips dumped into a mixing bowl and the dip still in its carton. Clark brought us our drinks. With the first sip of my Martini I felt myself unwinding from the long day. It was good to be with a group of friends with whom I didn't have to be on guard all the time. Even Clark seemed like just another government bureaucrat instead of a big shot at OSS.

'Before I forget,' Clark said, 'A friend of mine has been assigned out of town for a few months and he's given me the use of his little sailboat. It's moored on the Virginia side of the Potomac. If you like we could go out some Saturday and you girls can sunbathe while I fish.'

Curiouser and curiouser, I thought. Why was this man hanging out with us low-level government girls?

'That would be divine,' Sadie said. 'Can Peggy come too? Spencer works most weekends.'

'Of course,' Clark said.

This gave me an opening to ask about Peggy.

'Peggy's OK, isn't she?' I asked. 'I mean, she was so upset about Paul Hughes' death.'

'She's fine,' Rose said. 'She had to go to some important dinner with Spencer tonight.'

'She missed a fancy shindig at the Capital Yacht Club the Sunday Paul died. Told Spencer she didn't want to go. He was furious. They had a huge fight. I suppose she figured she'd better go with him tonight,' Sadie said.

Time to quiz Clark. 'Did you and Paul know each other?' I asked. 'I mean before the war.'

'Slightly,' Clark said. 'We were both at Yale. I was older than he but we lived in the same residence hall. In fact I provided a reference when he applied for his job here at OSS.'

'It was Clark who introduced us to Paul,' Sadie said. 'You would have liked Paul, Louise. He was smart and knowledgeable, he could talk about anything. I miss him.'

'It's a damn shame what happened,' Clark said.

'Save some of those for us,' Rose said, taking the bowl of chips away from Sadie and passing it around. 'Did you hear about what happened at the Little Palace Cafeteria yesterday?' she asked.

'Oh, yeah,' Sadie said. 'Three colored students from Howard University went into the place to get some sodas. The soda jerk served them, but when they went to pay at the register they were charged extra!' Another sit-in!

'Extra?' I said. 'What for?'

'For being colored,' Rose said.

'Sometimes I feel like this country still exists in the nineteenth century,' Clark said. 'When I lived in Paris such a thing would be unthinkable.'

'But you don't live in Paris anymore,' Sadie said.

'Sometimes I wish I still did. After the war, if things don't change here, I may move to Europe.'

I thought of Madeleine. In every way she was the equal of any white girl her age I knew, and she had more brains than many. I didn't see why she shouldn't get paid exactly the same as a white girl doing the same job, or why she was segregated at work. And why shouldn't she be able to buy a soda at a drug store or rent an apartment? When I was growing up in Wilmington I often wondered why the colored people accepted their lot so submissively. Of course I kept my mouth shut about what I thought.

The potato chips were gone so Sadie went into the kitchen and came back with a bowl of peanuts. 'This is it,' she said. 'The cupboard is bare.'

I'd finished my second drink and wondered if Clark was ready to leave. I caught his eye.

'I should really go,' Clark said. 'I need to prepare the notes I took today at the Conference for my secretary to type up tomorrow. Before I pick up Dr Soong in the morning.'

'I suppose you can't tell us all about him,' Sadie said.

'No I can't,' Clark said, standing up to leave. 'But I predict that China will be a major power someday. Now that it's a democracy all those people will control their own destiny.'

The small old man wearing a filthy raincoat and swigging on a bottle wrapped in a paper bag peered around the corner at the entrance to the apartment building. He ignored the stares of pedestrians passing by and fixed his eyes on the doorway. A couple came out; it was Leach and the girl. She had a nice figure and pretty hair, but she had to be at least thirty and wore round-rimmed spectacles. She was no knockout and not young, so she wouldn't stand out in a crowd; that was good. He watched Leach hand her into his car – such a gentleman – and drive off. Well, he'd wanted to see her face and now he had. He straightened up and walked off to the closest bus stop, throwing his paper bag into the nearest trashcan. When it hit bottom a Coke bottle slid out of the bag.

Clark stopped around the corner from my boarding house to drop me off. We'd agreed mutually that he'd never pick me up or drop me off where anyone would see us together. Perhaps he was sensitive about the difference in status between us. Just as well – I didn't want anyone to think I was dating him.

'Want to go to the movies tomorrow night?' he asked, after he'd come around to open my door. '*Mission to Moscow* is supposed to be even better than the book. Walter Huston plays Ambassador Davies.'

I was taken by surprise. There was not a romantic spark between us. I'd about given up trying to figure him out. Why not Rose or Sadie? He'd known them longer than he'd known me. Perhaps he just wanted to get away, and I was an undemanding companion.

'Sure,' I said. Why not?

Friday morning Milt shambled into the dining room in his pajamas and robe, unshaven.

Phoebe blanched. Ada, Henry and I focused on our breakfast, preparing for an unpleasant scene.

'Don't look at me like that,' Milt said to his mother.

'Honey, I just think you should dress before you come downstairs,' she said. 'That's all.'

'I had a bad night,' he said.

'Son,' Henry began.

'I am not your son!' Milt snapped at him.

'Sorry,' Henry said. 'It was just an expression.'

Silently Ada passed Milt the platter of pancakes and sausage. She held it for him so he could scrape his breakfast on to his plate with one hand.

'Where's the maple syrup?' he asked.

'There isn't any,' Phoebe said. 'We're using honey.'

Milt threw his fork on to the table. 'Damn it!' he said. 'You'd think Dellaphine had been cooking long enough to know not to fix pancakes when there's no maple syrup. Mother, get her to scramble some eggs for me, would you?'

Phoebe would stand up for Dellaphine under any circumstances, even to her son.

'Breakfast is over,' Phoebe said. 'Since the war came and there are more people in the house Dellaphine doesn't prepare individual breakfasts. She has too much else to do.'

'She'll do it for me if I ask her,' Milt said. He got up from his place and pushed through the swinging doors into the butler's pantry on his way to the kitchen. Phoebe put her head in her hands.

'Phoebe, he'll get better,' Ada said. 'He's been through so much.'

'He just needs some time,' Henry said. 'Maybe when his Purple Heart arrives it will perk him up.'

Phoebe nodded, pushing her plate – still full of food – away from her. It seemed to me that she'd gotten even thinner since Milt had come home.

'Excuse me,' Phoebe said. 'I'm going to fix Milt some eggs.'

She followed her son through the swinging doors.

'I would have thought Phoebe's son would be more of a man,' Henry said, his voice lowered almost to a whisper.

'You haven't been to war, have you?' Ada said.

'What do you mean by that?' Henry asked.

At this point I decided it was time to clear the table. I carried a stack of dirty dishes into the kitchen where I found Dellaphine filling the sink with suds while Phoebe broke eggs into the frying pan. Milt leaned back in a kitchen chair, his eyes closed.

'I'm going to feed the chickens before I leave for work,' I said. I'd settled the half-grown chicks into the coop outside yesterday. So I slipped down the kitchen steps to the back yard, where I found Madeleine under the stairs smoking a cigarette.

'You ran off,' I said. 'Coward.'

Madeleine was dressed in one of the suits Ada had given her last summer when she cleaned out her wardrobe, a chic khaki number with pink trim. I'd gotten some nice dresses at the same time. Both Madeleine and I joked we wanted Ada to gain more weight so we could rummage through her closet again.

'That kitchen wasn't big enough for all of us,' Madeleine said.

'Was Milt always like this?' I asked her.

Madeleine shook her head. 'Not at all,' she said. 'He used to be real nice to all of us. After Mr Holcombe died he sort of became the man of the house and he was very serious and responsible and kind to his mother.'

'I guess war changes people,' I said. 'And pain changes people too.'

Madeleine shrugged. 'All I know is, if he was a colored man, he would be back at work somewhere by now. He'd have to be. Otherwise he'd starve.'

'One of the men who works for my daddy has one leg,' I said. 'He gets along fine.'

Madeleine walked down to the chicken coop with me.

We watched the chicks run pell-mell to us, squawking and flapping their half-grown wings, as we scattered their feed.

'One of those chicks is a rooster,' Madeleine said. 'I can see a bitty comb.'

'First time he crows he goes in the pot,' I said.

'Did I ever tell you about my daddy?' she asked, out of the blue.

'No you never have,' I said. I had never pumped anyone at 'Two Trees' about Madeleine's father. It wasn't any of my business.

'He left us four years ago.'

'I'm so sorry,' I said.

'It wasn't like that,' she said, smiling at me. 'Daddy plays the piano almost as good as Cab Calloway, he really does. He used to play at church and he had a little group that did gigs a couple of nights a week. When the white men started to join the Army he got an offer from a good orchestra and he's been traveling with them ever since.'

The half-grown rooster butted the hens away from the food and raised his head, the muscles in his neck rippling. It wouldn't be long.

'He never comes home?' I couldn't help but ask.

'He and Momma don't speak. She wouldn't go with him. And she won't let him give her any money either. Momma thinks the only way for a colored person to be secure is to attach himself to some nice white family that will take care of him when he gets old. But Daddy plays at a "U" Street club sometimes and I get to see him when he's in town.'

Madeleine checked her watch, a cute twenty-four-hour Timex with an Air Force blue band.

'Lord,' she said, 'I need to go. I might miss my bus.'

'Madeleine,' I said, as I walked back to the house with her. 'Do you ever worry about what will happen after the war? I mean, if you'll be able to keep your job? After the men come home?'

'I expect I will,' she said. 'No white man wants to do what I do, punching out Social Security cards on that infernal machine, for the wages I get.'

I was concentrating so deeply on my work that when someone touched me on the shoulder I jumped.

'I didn't mean to startle you,' Spencer Benton said.

'It's OK,' I said. Benton had a notebook and pen clutched in one hand.

'Is there something you need?' I asked.

'No, no, nothing like that,' Benton said. 'I was wondering if we could have a cup of coffee together? There's something I want to talk with you about.'

'Of course,' I said, pushing my chair back from my little desk, so crowded with thick files, document stamps, a calendar, index cards and notepads that I barely had space to work. I'd been analyzing an intelligence document written in such tiny handwriting I'd needed a magnifying glass to read it. The notes had been scribbled on a playing card and concealed in a deck of cards that was smuggled out of Germany. I was getting a headache. A cup of coffee and a couple of aspirin were just what I needed.

But why did Spencer Benton want to talk with me? I barely knew the man.

It was a little late for coffee hour so the cafeteria was almost empty. We had a table to ourselves. Spencer stirred milk into his coffee. I wished I had more than one teaspoon of sugar in mine. I washed down my aspirin with a couple of gulps.

Spencer looked utterly careworn. Being exhausted was standard for us all, especially during the week, but he looked as though he hadn't slept in days. He kept stirring, as though postponing a conversation.

'I want to talk to you about something personal,' he said. 'Peggy. And those other girls, Rose and Sadie.'

'What about them?' I said.

'I want Peggy to stay away from them. And I think you should keep away from them, too.'

I bit my tongue. The idea that this man could tell me who my friends should be!

Or his wife's too, for that matter!

'They're pinko, you know,' he said.

'Really,' I said, trying to keep the irritation out of my voice.

'It reflects badly on me,' he said, 'for my wife to be friends with someone like Rose Dudley.'

'I don't see why,' I said.

'She was a reporter during the Spanish Civil War. She had an affair with Walter Roman, the Romanian Communist who fought in one of the International Brigades.'

Last I noticed it wasn't a crime to have an affair with someone who fought Franco. But I kept my mouth shut, just like always. 'She passed the OSS screening process, didn't she?' I said. OSS was fully staffed with Communists, anarchists, socialists, monarchists and God knew who else. There must be more to this than politics.

'That's not the point,' he said. 'I don't want her filling Peggy's head with all those crazy ideas about women's rights. She's my wife. It's OK for her to work now – we're at war – but afterwards she'll have plenty to do when I go back to Yale. We'll buy a nice house and we'll have to entertain a lot if I have a hope of being chairman of my department. We'll have kids too. She'll have more than enough to do.'

So that was it. Spencer was afraid Peggy was becoming too independent.

'I went to the Capital Yacht Club for an important reception a couple of weeks ago and she wouldn't go with me! Said she wanted her Sunday off for herself. She was going to the library! If she's not at Rose's apartment she's at the damn library. She's my wife, she should spend her time at home.'

'Spencer, I don't know Peggy well enough to talk to her

about something so personal. I need to get back to work,' I said. 'Thanks for the coffee.'

The audience stood as one and applauded. Many of us were crying. The Movietone newsreel had brought us all to our feet in a rush of emotion and optimism about the war. Footage of the victory parade in Tunis, accompanied by triumphant military music and Lowell Thomas's familiar voice, made patriotic goose bumps pop up and down my arms. The victorious generals, Monty, Ike and Andy, led the procession, followed by rank after rank of allied troops, including free French Arabs wearing their native clothing.

After the parade the newsreel switched topics to the first anniversary of the WAACs, showing us rank on rank of uniformed women marching in formation. If this wasn't enough to inspire our confidence in victory, the next few segments showed us the hundreds of tanks that were rolling off production lines, artillery practice off the California coast and a clip of Franklin Roosevelt and Winston Churchill sitting on the White House lawn, smiling and smoking equally large cigars, looking confident of victory.

The allies had won the Battle of the Atlantic and defeated the Axis powers in North Africa. The talk around OSS was that conquering Italy wouldn't be a big obstacle for the allies. Most Italians hated Mussolini and Hitler and were not about to die for them. The Germans were expected to abandon Italy and retreat to the north.

Invading Fortress Europe was the allies' next, massive, objective. Both Churchill and Roosevelt publicly agreed that it would take at least a year to prepare a cross-channel invasion.

Taking Italy would be a diversion, the means to take some of the pressure off the Soviet Union and the Second Front.

The newsreel switched to footage of waves of RAF bombers taking off from Malta, and I felt tears forming. My dear friend Rachel Bloch, a French Jew, had escaped with her children from southern France just days before the Germans occupied

Vichy Marseilles. She'd taken refuge in Malta. For a year Nazi bombers in Sicily and British bombers in Malta engaged in daily bombing of each other. I knew Rachel and her children were well. I had received several letters from her. What a relief it would be for her, and the rest of Malta, to see the Nazis driven from Sicily so they could enjoy quiet spring days on their battered but lovely island. Perhaps now I could get some relief packages to her.

Clark brought me out of my reverie by tapping my arm. 'Help me eat this popcorn,' he said. 'The movie's about to start.' The popcorn was good even though it was drenched in melted margarine instead of butter.

A very long hour and twenty minutes later the theater curtain closed and the lights came on to a smattering of applause.

'So, what did you think?' Clark said, as we jostled our way outside and through the throng of people waiting for the second show.

My instinct for self-preservation and job security kicked in. I wasn't about to tell him what I really thought. The movie was about the best example of white propaganda I had ever seen. I understood why the movie was made. The Soviet Union was our ally now, and it was important to rally a suspicious public around the alliance.

Without the Soviet Union tying up the Nazis on the Second Front, we probably wouldn't have been able to beat Rommel in North Africa. But for Walter Huston, who was playing Ambassador Davies, actually to stand up and declare that it was reasonable for Stalin to invade Finland, and to explain away the Party purges, was too much for me to accept. Without Spencer's help I had already figured out that Rose, Sadie and Clark, and probably the late Paul Hughes, were left-wingers. I wondered if they were sympathetic to the Communist movement. That was OK with me; lots of people at OSS were. I might be too, I suspected, if that meant being against segregation and for equal pay for women. But I wanted to keep my job so I measured my words carefully, just in case Clark was as loose-lipped at work as he was within our little group.

'The acting was really good,' I said.

'But the message was the most important thing,' Clark said. He opened the car door for me and I tucked my tailored skirt under me as I slid in. I hadn't had time to change from my work clothes.

'I see that,' I said carefully. 'The American public knows so little about the Soviet Union. And it's important that they understand why Stalin made a non-aggression pact with Hitler before the war started.'

Clark nodded. My answer had been sufficient.

He shifted his car into gear and we moved out into the crowded streets.

'How about a drink?' he asked.

'I'm sorry,' I said. 'Maybe some other time. I'm beat.'

First thing Saturday morning I hopped a bus to the Bureau of Engraving, but I had no intention of catching a streetcar. When I got off the bus, directly ahead of me to the south was the Tidal Basin, but I turned north on 'D', past the Department of Agriculture, an annex and a heating plant. I turned on to 12th Street and found the Western Union office.

Inside controlled bedlam reigned. A long counter stretched across the front of the office.

Four girls helped customers who waited in long lines with their telegraph forms already filled out. The girls took the customers' money and recorded the transaction in a ledger. In the back of the store the telegraph operators, all men, clacked continuously, sending telegrams as fast as they could from the stacks of forms the girls put into their in-boxes. They wore earphones or they couldn't possibly have concentrated well enough to tap out the dots and dashes correctly. In another part of the office several women, also wearing earphones, pulled strips of paper out of teletype machines, glued them to telegram forms and handed them to one of a score of boys in caps and worn shoes to deliver. Another man sat at a switchboard receiving telegram requests by phone from customers with accounts. It was a remarkable system, really. You could communicate with anyone in the world within minutes.

I waited patiently in line until it was my turn at the counter.

A young girl with blonde wavy hair styled like Barbara Stanwyck's waited on me.

'Can I help you?' she asked.

'Yes,' I said. I pulled a badge out of my pocketbook, a District Police badge, number twenty-three, issued to Donna Munro. 'I'm a policewoman,' I said. Apparently Miss Munro owed Detective Royal a favor – a really big one – and allowed him to borrow her badge on her day off.

The telegraph girl, whose name was Minnie according to her name badge, slapped her hand over her mouth. When her surprise abated she removed her hand and said, 'I didn't know girls could work for the police.'

'Sure,' I said. 'There are almost a hundred of us.' Now, District policewomen only did chores like guarding arrested women and caring for lost children and such, but Minnie didn't need to know that.

'I think that's grand!' Minnie said. 'Are you investigating something?'

'Yes, I am,' I said. 'I need to find out the return address on a telegram we have as evidence in a case. We know it was sent from this office. The return address wasn't printed on the telegram. I was wondering if you kept a record of it anyway?'

'Oh, yes!' Minnie breathed. 'In case a customer's check bounces or something! Do you have our code from the telegram?'

'I do,' I said, and recited it to her from memory.

Minnie wrote down the code on the back of a telegraph form and hurried over to a nearby door. When she opened it I saw shelves of canvas ledgers stacked one on top of the other.

She went inside, and when she returned she handed me a scrap of paper with the address – 710 'E' Street SW. Maybe ten blocks from where I was standing.

'Thank you,' I said, 'this will be so helpful.'

Minnie clasped her hands in front of her and, still breathless, said, 'Can you tell me if you're investigating, well, a murder? Like Ellery Queen!'

I wanted to make Minnie happy, but I just couldn't.

'I can't say, ma'am,' I said. 'Regulations.'

I walked north toward the address Minnie gave me and shortly found myself in a street lined with tiny storefronts. I passed a laundry with a sign that read 'No New Customers' out front, and a café with a hand-lettered note taped to the front door that read 'Help Wanted, Colored May Apply', before I found myself in front of the address I was looking for, a newsagent with a sign over the door that read 'Zruchat's News and Sundries'. Another door next to the entrance to the store led to a staircase going up to the second floor. The door was locked. An American flag placard rested in one of the two windows. I shivered despite the warm day. Whoever sent the telegram that claimed Hughes was ill might live in the rooms over the shop. I might be one move away from solving the mystery of his death.

An old-fashioned bell over the door tinkled when I entered the store.

The shop couldn't have been more than ten feet square. It was packed with cheap merchandise. There was a rack of magazines, newspapers and comic books. A shelf crowded with sundries like aspirin and mouthwash and safety pins. A short counter stretched along the back. Dusty canned goods and beer bottles lined the shelves behind it.

A small man sat on a stool behind the counter. He was hunched over like an old man but his face was smooth and unlined. His stone grey hair hung long, reaching down to his collar in back but pushed neatly behind his ears. His faded blue eyes were huge behind thick round spectacles.

'Good afternoon, madam,' he said in a heavy Russian accent.

'Good afternoon,' I said to him, stretching my hand over

the counter to shake his. It was surprisingly firm for an old man.

'What can I get for you today?' he asked.

'I'm not actually shopping,' I said. 'I'm from the Western Union Company. My name is Patsy Mason.' Really, Sergeant Royal should work for OSS. He'd given me great cover identities.

'And I am Lieb Zruchat,' he said. 'I am a shopkeeper, as you can see. So what does a great company like Western Union want with me?'

I leaned on the counter and pretended to refer to a small notebook I'd pulled out of my pocketbook.

'I'm conducting a survey of our customers,' I said. 'Do you mind answering a few questions about our service?'

Zruchat shifted on his stool and grimaced, clutching his back.

'Apologies,' he said. 'An old war injury, from an old war! The Great War. Now we got another one, we call the first World War One.' He rolled his eyes. 'What,' he said, 'will there be a World War Three? Only after I am dead, I hope. But lady,' he continued, 'I have never sent a telegram. Not ever in my life.'

'It could have been the person who lives upstairs,' I said.

'Lady, the person who lives upstairs is me. And my cat Leo.'

'Really?' I said, glancing down at my notebook prop. 'But according to my notes you sent a telegram very recently. A couple of weeks ago.'

Zruchat shook his head emphatically. 'No, lady,' he said. 'I got a telephone.' He nodded at the antiquated instrument sitting on the shelf behind him. 'Why spend a dime if I can just call?'

'You're sure?' I asked.

'Of course,' he said. 'I know if I send a telegram or not.'

'Well, it must be a mistake, then,' I said. 'I'm sorry to have bothered you.'

He shrugged. 'Time I got. No customers will come this time of day.' He pointed to the magazine rack. 'Don't you want the new issue of *Photoplay*? All about George Stevens in *The More the Merrier*.'

'No thanks,' I said. I felt guilty for lying to the man, who was obviously not involved in the Hughes case. Which was becoming murkier by the minute. 'But I'll take a Baby Ruth.' He handed me the candy bar and I gave him a nickel. The bell above the door tinkled again as I left.

I felt deflated as I stood at the bus stop waiting to go back into Washington. The inquiry had reached a dead end. Obviously whoever had really sent the telegram had just grabbed an address on a nearby street out of thin air to use as the return address on the telegram. Or perhaps the person had passed by Mr Zruchat's shop on the way to the telegraph office and remembered the address.

So many events related to Hughes' murder had taken place within such a small area. Paul Hughes died and was found in the Tidal Basin. A streetcar terminus which connected the area to the entire city was just across the street. A telegram was sent from the nearest Western Union office claiming that Hughes was ill, using the address of an old Russian's pitiful little shop a few streets away. Was this all coincidence, or did it mean something?

If Paul Hughes was ill, why did he go back to his boarding house? Why didn't he take a taxi instead of walking? Who sent the telegram? A girlfriend who wanted to stay anonymous? Why did Paul leave if she gave him an excuse to stay? Or was there a girlfriend at all, or something much more malicious going on? Was it 'G' who sent the telegram?

I wondered what Sergeant Royal would do next.

SIX

Give every girl an adequate number of rest periods during the day. [. . .] you have to make some allowance for feminine psychology. A girl has more confidence and consequently is more efficient if she can keep her hair tidied, apply fresh lipstick and wash her hands several times a day.
'1943 Guide to Hiring Women', *Mass Transportation* magazine, July 1943.

I t was quiet inside the house. If anyone was home they must be napping, which sounded like a wonderful idea to me. If I couldn't fall asleep I could finish *Hungry Hill*.

Just in case Phoebe was asleep I tiptoed up the stairs, my shoes in hand. When I got to the second floor landing a voice called down to me from the third floor. It was Milt.

'Who's there?' he called out.

'Hush!' I said. 'You'll wake up your mother!'

'She could sleep through a hurricane,' Milt said from the top of the stairs.

She probably could, especially if she'd taken a Nembutal. Milt's head poked around the banister.

'I've got some new records', he said. 'Come listen to them with me.'

I didn't have the heart to turn him down. I'd never been in the men's attic bedroom before. Joe had shared it with Henry before he left for New York. We often communicated by knocking on a metal pipe that passed through our rooms. A pang of sadness struck me. Joe would never live here again. I clung to the thought that when – or if – he returned to the District he'd find lodging that would permit us a few hours of privacy occasionally. It occurred to me that one reason I postponed visiting him in New York was the chance that we'd never have an entire weekend to ourselves again, and we'd be even unhappier than we were now!

The attic room was more attractive than I expected. The dark ceiling beams were high overhead and a ceiling fan turned slowly under them. It would get too hot in summer to sleep there – Joe and Henry always moved to the porch. A curtain separated Milt's sleeping area from Henry's.

Milt was sprawled out on a double bed propped up on pillows and cushions. He was dressed in khakis and a plaid sport shirt but his feet were bare. Today's newspaper and a couple of western paperbacks were spread out around him. A half empty bottle of bourbon sat on a table next to the bed, which also held a lamp and a record player.

'Come into my lair,' he said, and tossed me a couple of pillows. I sat cross-legged at the foot of his bed.

'You look comfortable,' I said, 'like a sheikh in his tent.'

'So where are the dancing girls?' he asked. He seemed to me less angry than he had been this morning. That might be the bourbon, though.

'Want a swig?' he asked, passing me the bottle of bourbon.

'Sure,' I said, taking the bottle and swallowing a couple of gulps.

'My goodness, the lady likes her liquor,' he said, taking the bottle back from me and taking another pull himself.

'Have you been up here all day?' I asked.

'Yes,' he said. 'Hiding out from my mother and Henry. But I just started drinking an hour or so ago.'

'You've made quite a dent in that bottle in an hour,' I said.

'It wasn't full when I started.' Milt raised the bottle to his lips and then offered it to me again.

'No thanks,' I said.

'Henry was pestering me about when I was going to get my Purple Heart and I couldn't stand it.'

'Henry admires you,' I said.

'He admires soldiers,' he said. 'He doesn't know me from Adam. I'm not a hero.'

'I think most of us think anyone who has been through what you have is a hero,' I said.

Milt, cradling his bottle of bourbon, regarded me with a speculative expression on his face.

'Can you keep a secret?' he asked.

'I'm an expert at it,' I said.

'This isn't a war wound,' he said. 'I won't be getting a goddamned Purple Heart for it. Some of my buddies and me lifted a case of beer from a Quonset supply hut when we were on leave and tried to outrun the MPs in a jeep. We "borrowed" the jeep by hot-wiring it, by the way. We hit a huge pothole and I got tossed out of the jeep and landed in the road. My buddy who was driving backed over me. Goodbye arm. And you know what? Not only am I not getting any medals, but I'm afraid my discharge papers are going to read "dishonorable". Fat chance I'll get a job with that hanging over my head.'

'I am so sorry,' I said. 'But—'

'Don't start,' he said, swigging from the bottle again. 'It was just an accident, right? My glass is half full, right? It could have been my right arm, right? Look, I heard all that from the chaplain about a hundred times.'

'You didn't listen to him, did you?' I said, getting off the bed and smoothing down my skirt.

'Don't go,' Milt said, sitting up and swinging his legs off the side of the bed. 'We haven't listened to the records yet. Please.'

Until now I had thought of Milt as just an unpleasant complication to my life at 'Two Trees'. But now I caught myself feeling sorry for him.

'Stop drinking?' I asked.

'Sure,' he said, corking the bourbon bottle and setting it on the floor beside him.

I sat back down on the bed while he cued up the needle on one of his new records. We shared a compatible half hour listening to the Mills Brothers and Glenn Miller. I almost offered to go down to my room and get some of my Carter Family records, but he probably disliked hillbilly music.

'So how should I tell Mother?' Milt asked, returning to the

subject of his accident. 'And what do I tell Henry about the Purple Heart?'

'If it were me, I would lie,' I said.

Milt was shocked by my answer. 'It didn't occur to me that you would suggest such a thing,' he said.

'The truth would upset your mother terribly. You had an accident and you've paid for your poor judgment in full. It could have happened to any number of sailors on a shore leave toot. You were thousands of miles away fighting a war where you could have been killed any day. It's nobody's business what happened but yours.'

'I really don't have to tell her?'

'Hell no.'

'What about Henry? He's pestering me to death for all the heroic details.'

'Henry is a jackass. Make something up and then forget about it. After the war is over he'll go home and be out of your life.'

Milt looked at his empty sleeve. 'I guess it could be worse,' he said.

'It can always be worse,' I said.

Sunday morning, while Phoebe and Dellaphine were at church, Ada and I were making biscuits for us all when Henry poked his head through the door. 'Phone call, Louise. It's Joe, long distance.'

I felt the heat rush into my face and prayed Ada and Henry wouldn't see how thrilled I was. I think Ada knew our feelings for each other, but Henry was purely ignorant and I wanted to keep it that way.

'Say hello to Joe for me,' Ada said, smiling widely as she said it. She knew. But I could count on her to keep our secret. Lord knows I was keeping a big one for her.

'Don't tell Henry,' I said, wiping my hands on a dishtowel.

'What do you take me for?'

Henry was in the lounge reading the Sunday *Washington Times-Herald* when I reached the telephone table in the hall. I was afraid he could hear me so I cupped my hand over the receiver.

'Hello?' I said.

'Hello, darling,' Joe said. Oh God, I wished he wouldn't call me that!

'How are you?' I asked.

'I miss you.'

'Me too.'

'Can you talk?'

'Sort of.'

'Listen, Louise, I don't have a room-mate. No one knows you in New York. Come visit me, please! We can be alone and no one will know. Please!'

I glanced toward the open lounge door. Henry had turned on the radio to the news.

'I would love to, Joe. I would love to!'

'There's a train that leaves Union Station at five minutes past six every Friday. Send me a telegram and I'll be waiting for you at Grand Central at eleven. Please come.'

'I'll manage it somehow,' I said.

I could tell by the tone of his voice that he was surprised.

'Really! When?' he said.

'I don't know,' I said. 'Soon.' I could tell everyone I was visiting my parents in Wilmington.

'Until then,' he said.

After I hung up the receiver, heart pounding, Henry came out into the hall.

'Was that Joe?' Henry asked. 'Does he know yet when he'll be back in the District?'

From his oblivious expression I figured Henry didn't hear the gist of our conversation.

'No, not yet,' I said.

'If Milt stays here, I suppose Joe'll have to find someplace else to live when he does get back,' Henry said.

'I suppose he will.' I shrugged, hoping to give the impression that Joe's housing dilemma didn't matter to me.

I told Ada and Phoebe that I was walking over to a filling station for a cold Coke from their red ice chest. I got the Coke, but then I ducked around the corner into the alley where I'd arranged to meet Sergeant Royal. He was already waiting for me, sitting on a wooden box smoking a cigarette.

He pulled another box up to his as if it were a chair cozied up to a fireplace and asked, 'Won't you join me?'

'Lovely weather today, isn't it?' I said. 'So nice for an afternoon stroll.'

I sat down and stretched out trousered legs. He offered me a cigarette and I refused.

'So, what did you find out?' he asked.

I crossed my arms. I was determined to get myself out of this.

'Something very interesting,' I said.

'What?' he asked. 'Tell me!'

'On one condition,' I said.

He shook his head. 'Sorry, Mrs Pearlie, I don't do conditions.'

'I want you to leave me alone from now on.'

'I can't promise that. I might need you again.'

'You must have other people who can run your errands for you.'

Royal grinned and shook his head. 'Not without attracting the attention of my superiors,' he said, 'and not as smart as you are. Listen, Mrs Pearlie, Paul Hughes was murdered. Don't you feel any responsibility to help find his murderer? And if not responsibility, curiosity?'

I waited until two chatting women pushing baby carriages strolled well past the opening to the alley to answer him.

'I don't want to lose my job,' I said.

Royal turned his cigarette lighter, an ancient Zippo with most of the plating worn off, around in his hands.

'Let's compromise,' he said. 'You tell me what you know, and I'll tell you more about the case. And I won't report you to your bosses. I reserve the right to ask you to help me again. But you can say no.'

'Sounds as complicated as an international treaty,' I said.

'It's all I got,' he said.

'OK,' I said. I waited again, until a family that looked like mother, father, daughter and daughter's kids, all dressed in Sunday clothes, passed by the alley. They seemed quite somber. Daughter's husband must be in the military. Or deceased.

'The covers you provided me worked wonderfully,' I said. 'I went to the Western Union office and completely convinced one of clerks that I was a policewoman. She gave me the return address associated with the telegram Mrs Nighy received, the one that was supposedly from Hughes' mother.'

Royal gripped my arm with excitement. 'You went to the address, didn't you?'

'Yes, but it was a disappointment. It's the address of a tiny news and sundries shop,' I said. 'It's run by an old Russian guy. He lives in the apartment upstairs. So it seems that whoever sent the telegram just picked an address nearby.'

Royal covered his mouth with his hand, thinking. 'Let's say that Hughes had a girlfriend. When he became ill, she sent a telegram to Mrs Nighy pretending to be his mother. Using a phoney address on the form, an address that just happened to be occupied by your elderly Russian shopkeeper. Maybe she passed by it every day. But Hughes was determined to get back to his boarding house and his work. So he left his girl-friend's place before he should have, collapsed, hit his head and fell into the Tidal Basin and drowned? I just don't believe it. Why would all his identification be missing? That points to homicide. But if there is a girlfriend, what, if anything, did she have to do with his murder?'

I thought of 'G' and the meeting he had with Hughes on Sunday, when Hughes was supposed to be at his mother's but wasn't. Was 'G' a girlfriend? Or a barber? Or a bookie? Or was 'G' a person related to Hughes' work at OSS? And why did Major Wicker want me to check out the files Hughes was reading? Did Hughes' death have anything to do with those files? Why did OSS send Hughes' personnel file to the Limited file room? If it was so clear to Royal that Hughes' death was a homicide, why had OSS hushed it up? Was it just to keep the police and the FBI out of OSS business? If so, were the OSS still investigating, despite what they said?

I couldn't tell Sergeant Royal about 'G'. I just couldn't. It was my responsibility to lead him away from anything that might involve OSS.

'You seem sure that Hughes had a girlfriend, and that his weekends away from Mrs Nighy were to spend time with her,' I said. 'But you don't know that; there could be another explanation, couldn't there?'

'Oh,' Royal said, 'he had a girlfriend all right. I told you I had some information for you.'

'What?' I said.

'I put an advertisement in the personal section of the newspaper pretending to be a private detective looking for a philanderer. I asked if any landlord in the District rented living space to a man who might be using it sometimes to meet a girl.'

'You must have gotten hundreds of responses,' I said.

'Not at all,' Royal said. 'How many rooms in the District are occupied part-time? The Housing Authority would slap the owner with a fine in a minute.' True, I thought. At 'Two Trees' we worried that someday the Housing Authority would find out that Ada and I had our own rooms and insist that Phoebe house two more women.

Royal popped a couple of aspirin, dry, before continuing.

'So I called them all, and by God, a woman who runs a residential hotel not that far from Mrs Nighy described Hughes down to a T. Said he called himself Anderson. This Anderson told her that his business brought him to town often and that he was tired of trying to find a hotel room. And then she told me that a girl visited him regularly.'

'OK,' I said. 'So he had a girlfriend. What does that have to do with his death?'

'I don't know. But this hotel is just a few blocks away from Mrs Nighy's.'

He pulled out an Esso map of Washington to show me. I knew the neighborhood fairly well myself. It was just a few blocks from Rose's and Peggy's apartments. The area was teeming with government employees lodged in private homes, apartments and hotels.

'Look,' I said, 'this hotel is not that far from Mrs Nighy's, way to the northwest of the Tidal Basin. If he was taken ill there he wouldn't be traveling by way of the Tidal Basin to get home. He must have been coming from somewhere else.'

'And the Tidal Basin is across the street from the streetcar terminus at the Bureau of Engraving,' Royal said. 'And the Western Union office and the return address of the phoney telegram are within walking distance.'

God, I thought, how could anyone solve a puzzle like this with so many pieces missing?

'So Hughes could have been coming from anywhere,' I said.

'Just about,' Royal said. He folded up the map and tucked it into his pocket.

'Remind me why you want to find the girlfriend?'

'The more we know about Hughes' life the more likely it is we can find his murderer. She might know what he was doing over the weekend and where he was.'

'How are you going to find her?' I asked.

'This is where you come in,' he said.

I didn't even object. But I did check my watch.

'Tell me,' I said. 'I've got to go soon.'

'Go over to that hotel,' he said. 'Snoop around. First make sure that Anderson was Hughes. I've got a copy of his government ID picture. Don't ask me how I got it, I can't tell you. Ask questions if you can. People don't suspect women much.'

'I'll go when I can,' I said. 'Maybe at lunch tomorrow.'

I stood up and brushed the wrinkles out of my dress. Royal handed me the passport-sized photo of Hughes. He stood, but his bad leg buckled and he had to brace himself against the wall of the alley.

'I hope the war ends soon,' he said. 'I can't do this much longer.'

*   *   *

I just barely made it to my desk by nine o'clock, the last possible minute I could arrive at work without being reported for tardiness to my boss. In fact, Mr Shera found me shortly after I sat down to organize my day.

'Louise,' he said.

'Yes, sir,' I answered, ready for him to assign me some mundane dusty task amongst the files.

'You're wanted by Mr Lewis again,' he said. Shera looked annoyed that I had been drawn away from my work yet again.

So I found myself hustling across 'E' Street and up the three flights of steps in the main OSS building. Lewis's disapproving secretary was not at her desk. I knocked on Lewis's door. Major Wicker answered.

Major Wicker showed me to one of the club chairs.

'Mrs Pearlie,' Wicker said. 'I have one more little job for you. Take your lunch hour so as not to arouse suspicion.' He handed me a scrap of paper with an address on it. The address of the residential hotel where Paul Hughes lived under his other identity!

So OSS had been following the same line of inquiry as Sergeant Royal. And this must mean that they too were suspicious of Hughes' 'accidental' death, even though OSS had accepted and disseminated the story inside the agency. Interesting. Did OSS agree with Royal? Did Wicker believe too that Paul Hughes had been murdered?

'It seems,' Wicker said, 'that Paul Hughes lived another life. He rented a room as a Mr Anderson. I want to know why. Poke around. Find out what you can. People are less reserved with a girl than they are with a man.'

'All right,' I said, pretending to memorize an address I already knew. I handed the scrap of paper back to Wicker. He lit it with his cigarette lighter and let it burn to cinders in the ashtray on the table.

'Report back to me when you're done,' Wicker said. 'Then Mr Shera can have you back. He's quite annoyed with me.'

Wicker gave me money for the taxi and I signed the receipt, which read 'reimbursement for office supplies'.

As I hurried back across the street the absurdity of all this crashed down upon me. I felt like a double agent. What if Wicker found out that I was working for Sergeant Royal too? It wouldn't impress him that I was keeping as much from Royal as I could. My career, such as it was, would be over. No matter how fascinating Hughes' death investigation was, after I reported to Wicker I would hide myself in the Registry for the rest of the war. And after I fed the same information to Royal I would refuse any more contact with him.

At lunchtime I wrapped myself in an old raincoat I kept at the office in case I was surprised by the weather. I pulled a straw fedora over my eyes. Too bad I didn't have my sunglasses, I thought, then my transformation into spy and snitch would be complete!

The taxi let me off on the corner across the street from my destination on New Hampshire. Paul Hughes' secret life took place in a nondescript four-story building with the words 'Worth's Residential Hotel' stenciled in black on a window on the ground floor. I circled the building, noting two doors and a fire escape – three entrances or exits for spies or lovers.

An ugly clanging signaled my entry into the building. The hall was clean but needed painting and the carpet was worn. A long sofa slipcovered in a fake tapestry print was the only furniture in the hall. The impressions of many pairs of buttocks showed on the cushions.

A window in the wall near me slid open, startling me.

A woman in a blue denim coverall and a grubby do-rag leaned out of it.

'What can I do for you, missy?' she said. 'We just rent to men here and we're full.'

'I'm not looking for a room,' I said. 'I'm looking for my brother.'

'Sure you are,' she said. 'You can tell me the truth. You got a boyfriend lives here?'

'No, really,' I said. 'I'm Mary Anderson. I'm looking for

my brother. I haven't heard from him in ages. I was in town and thought I'd come by. Is he here?'

'I don't know,' she said, unfolding a rectangle of chewing gum and popping it into her mouth. 'It's not my job to keep track of all these men. But Mr Anderson, he's not here much. Mostly on the weekends.'

'He lives in Fredericksburg,' I said. 'He rented this room to use when he's in town on business. The hotels are always full.'

'Well,' she said, chewing vigorously on her gum, 'I don't know if he's here, but you're welcome to go on up and see. Second floor at the end of the hall, room Two G.'

The second-floor hallway was much like the lobby. Clean, but in need of paint and new carpeting. I knocked on the door of room 2G, expecting no answer and getting none. I peered through the keyhole but saw nothing but the footboard of an iron bed and a tattered chenille bedspread.

I jiggled the doorknob and knocked again, just for appearances' sake.

Back downstairs I approached the custodian again.

I leaned into her window.

'Ma'am,' I said.

She was curled up in an armchair listening to the radio. 'What?' she said, without rising.

'Could I ask you just one more question?'

Sighing, she uncoiled herself and approached the window. 'What is it?' she asked.

I leaned over until our heads were close together.

'You see, my best friend Claire is engaged to my brother. She's heard so little from him recently that, well, she wondered if he's seeing someone here? Have you seen him with a girl?'

'Now, you know, the men here aren't supposed to bring in girls. But if they're quiet, and slip me a dollar, I don't mind. What they do is none of my business.'

I took the hint, found one of Wicker's dollars in my pocketbook and handed it over to her. She stuck it in her coverall pocket.

'You tell your friend that Mr Anderson has a girlfriend.'

'You're sure?'

'Course, I ain't blind. When he's here she comes over. All covered up in a trench coat and an ugly black scarf with yellow flowers, no matter what the weather is.'

'What does she look like?'

'Can't tell. I told you, she wears a scarf. She's got a nice figure.'

'Poor Claire!'

'Mr Anderson has other friends who visit him, too.'

'Really?'

'Yeah, couple men, couple women. But they don't come as often as the girlfriend.'

'Is there anything else you can tell me? Would you recognize the friends if you saw them?'

'Nah,' she said. 'All the men who live here got friends who drop by. I don't pay no attention to them. Like I said, if they're quiet so my boss doesn't hear about it I don't care.'

Major Wicker had arranged for us to meet outside of OSS at a drug store fountain across the street from George Washington University. It was a student hang-out, but students these days were older and often wearing military uniforms.

Stopping inside the door I removed my scarf and tucked it in my raincoat pocket. Then I spotted Wicker at the last booth. He was wearing civilian clothes, a double-breasted suit that disguised his girth. As I walked toward him I was sure the bulge under his armpit was his sidearm. The man must sleep with it.

Wicker stood up as I slid into the booth opposite him.

'How did it go?' he asked, before he even finished sitting down again.

'That depends on what you expected,' I said.

The soda jerk, who must have been at least sixty, appeared at our table with his pad and pencil.

'What would you two like for lunch today?' he asked.

'Got hamburgers?' Wicker asked.

'No sir.'

'OK,' Wicker said. 'Two hot dogs with mustard, catsup and onions. French fries. And coffee, black.'

'I'll have a bowl of chilli with saltines and a glass of milk,' I said.

'Bowl of red,' the jerk said to himself as he wrote down my order.

'Tell me what happened,' Wicker said once the waiter had left the table.

'The custodian said that Anderson, or rather Hughes, did have a girlfriend. A woman who visited him alone and often.'

'What did she look like?'

'She was always bundled up, hair under a scarf, dark glasses,' I answered. 'The custodian said that Hughes had other visitors too, men and women, but that they came less frequently than the woman she figured was his girlfriend.'

The soda jerk arrived with our food. I didn't realize how hungry I was until he set down the bowl of steaming chilli. There wasn't much meat in it but it tasted delicious to me, full of red beans and onions.

'You must want to know what is going on,' Wicker said.

'Of course,' I said.

'In no way did Hughes' job at OSS require him to acquire another identity and rent a room,' Wicker said. 'So he either wanted to conduct a romantic affair secretly . . .' Wicker didn't finish the sentence. But I knew what had to follow. Hughes could have been spying for another country. That's why Wicker had me find out what files Hughes was reading in the Reading Room. And why his personnel file had been moved to the restricted 'L' room.

The soda jerk cleared our table and we both ordered coffee. When he brought our cups to us he gave me one lump of sugar, one less than I would have liked to have, but I was grateful for it.

Wicker leaned over the cracked Formica and pursed his lips, looking at me as though he wanted to confide in me. And I wanted him to. At this point in time I was so desperately

curious about Hughes I'd almost have been willing to lose my
job to find out what the hell was going on. I took a chance
and asked him a question.

'Do you think Paul Hughes was compromising OSS
security?' I asked. 'And that he was murdered because of it?'

'I don't know yet, Mrs Pearlie, but if I could find this
girlfriend of his I believe she could answer many of our
questions.'

As I waited in line for the bus an old Ford Woody drove up
and stopped at the curb next to me.

'Lady,' the man at the wheel called out to me, 'want a ride?'
It was common for drivers to pick up government employees
at bus stops and offer rides, but I didn't want to go with a
stranger alone. I leaned over to look inside the narrow window.
It was Sergeant Royal with his fedora pulled down low over
his face.

I opened the car door.

'I didn't think you'd want me to pick you up here in a police
vehicle, so I drove my old bucket. Have a seat.'

When I saw the stained upholstery I hesitated to sit down.

'It's as clean as I can get it,' Royal said. 'There's a towel
in back if you want to cover the seat with that.' I did. After I
retrieved the towel and spread it on the seat I sat down and
closed the door. Rusty hinges made a scraping sound.

Royal pulled away from the curb and out into the usual
traffic jam.

'I bought this car in 1931,' he said. 'I was fixing to buy a
new one a year ago but then the Japs bombed Pearl Harbor
and all the car companies were switched over to military
vehicles. I'm just hoping I can keep this bucket running a
while longer.'

We crawled north on 21st Street toward my boarding house,
driving through the middle of the George Washington University
campus, which made me think of Joe. Teaching Slavic
languages there had been his cover story.

'Tell me,' Royal said.

I told him exactly what I had told Wicker. The absurdity of briefing both men with the same information on the same day did not escape me. I couldn't keep this up, despite my curiosity about Hughes. I was just asking for OSS to find out about my association with Royal and send me packing.

'We need to find the girlfriend,' Royal said, stopping at the intersection of 'I' Street to allow a gaggle of government workers to cross the street.

'You need to find her,' I said. 'I'm done.'

'Come on,' he said. 'You want the answers to Hughes' murder as badly as I do.'

'I'll just have to read about it in the papers,' I said.

Royal turned down a side street and parked in front of a vacant lot.

'What's this?' I said.

Royal turned to me. 'You remember I said I'd share information with you, too?'

'Yes,' I said. What had he found?

Royal pulled something out of his pocket and dropped it in my lap. It was a man's wallet. 'This isn't Hughes' wallet!' I said.

'Look inside,' he said.

I did. It was Hughes' wallet all right. Hughes' driver's license was inside, as was his draft card (stamped 'II-A' – exempted because of necessary civilian occupation), a couple of receipts and four dollars.

'Where did you find it?' I asked, handing the wallet back to Royal.

'A park ranger who oversees the Tidal Basin area called me this morning. I'd left a business card with him. Someone found the wallet under a park bench and turned it in.'

'You're kidding!' I said. 'It's been there all this time?'

'No,' he said, shaking his head. 'It would have been found by now, as busy as the Tidal Basin area is.' He turned the thin beige wallet over and over in his hands. 'The person who murdered Hughes planted it there. Recently. Like in the last couple of days.'

My skin crawled just thinking about the killer wandering

around the Tidal Basin until no one was in sight, then dropping the wallet.

'I don't understand why,' I said.

'He's hoping that we'll think Hughes simply lost the wallet. Which would support the notion that Hughes' death was an accident, that he hadn't been deliberately stripped of his identification. I'm sure my superiors will buy into that explanation. After I've dropped you off I'll take the wallet to my precinct, where it will join the other evidence in Hughes' closed file.'

I couldn't take my eyes off the wallet. 'What are you going to do now?' I asked.

'Try to convince you to help me find Hughes' girlfriend.'

'No,' I said. 'I can't get further involved in this. I just can't.'

Royal didn't argue with me. He stopped at Washington Square so I could walk to 'Two Trees'. By the time I got inside the door my nerves were jangling. I sank into the hall chair. Henry heard me and came out of the lounge.

'Are you OK?' he asked. 'You look done in.'

I was done, all right.

'I'm OK, just tired.'

He shrugged and went back inside the lounge.

I dragged myself upstairs and made myself a very strong Martini. I trusted Royal not to involve me now, no matter what happened. I might be in the clear.

After another Martini I went downstairs to dinner, where we all feasted on Dellaphine's chicken pot pie. It was one of my favorite meals even before rationing began.

Milt wasn't at dinner. I hesitated to ask about him, but Phoebe volunteered.

'I'm so pleased,' she said. 'Milt went out with some friends from college who heard he was in town. They're going to have drinks and dinner at the Metro Club. One of his friends' father is a member.'

'That's great news,' Henry said. 'He should get back out into the real world. Lots of veterans have bad war wounds. He needs to snap out of it.'

'I don't think it's that easy,' I said. 'None of us can understand what he's been through.'

'It's a first step,' Phoebe said. And indeed Phoebe herself looked much better. She had some color in her cheeks and ate most of her dinner.

I didn't spend the evening in the lounge with the others. I was worn out and felt a headache under way. It felt to me as if the weather was changing. Another spring thunderstorm must be on its way.

The next morning I was the last to get to the dining room, only to see Milt there, working his way through a plate of eggs and bacon. He was dressed and shaved.

'Want me to butter your toast, dear?' Phoebe asked.

'No thanks, I need to learn to do it myself,' Milt said. Using the side of the plate to brace one edge of the toast, he gently spread it with butter. Once the toast slid off the plate, but he just smiled. 'Butter side up,' he said, replacing the toast on the plate and finishing the job.

I wondered what had happened to cheer Milt up. I found out when he followed me into the hall and insisted on helping me with my coat. 'This is something else I need to learn to do,' he said. 'Must impress the ladies!' Then he whispered into my ear. 'I got my papers yesterday,' he said. 'I got an honorable discharge! I don't know why, but I am not protesting.'

'I'm so glad, Milt,' I said.

'Now I have a chance to make something of my life,' he said. 'I'll pick up a Purple Heart at a pawn shop to make Henry happy.'

I felt like a new person at work. Now that I was relieved of the pressure of Royal's threat to report me to OSS I felt like my old self. I applied myself with vigor to summarizing a twenty-page report on the movements of a fleet of Nazi tanks at a base in France. At night the young French woman who cleaned the nearby German barracks climbed over the ten-foot wire fence to record the serial numbers and odometer readings of all the tanks parked there. Much of the report was in French, but it was basic enough that my high school French was adequate to the task.

Tired of the OSS cafeteria I'd brought a cheese and pickle sandwich and a thermos of milk from home so I could spend my lunch hour outside in the warm spring air. I leaned my back up against a tall sugar maple drooping with clusters of chartreuse flowers and gazed south-east toward the Tidal Basin. I couldn't see it, but I could picture it surrounded by cherry trees in full leaf. Such irony, that it was one of the prettiest parts of the District due to a gift from the Japanese government. True, that gift was made over thirty years ago, but still. I wondered if after the war the United States would ever have cordial relations with Japan again. It seemed doubtful to me.

I was watching the horizon darken over the Potomac, a harbinger of that spring thunderstorm I suspected was on its way, when Clark Leach spoke to me.

'I'm intruding on your lunch hour,' he said.

'It's OK,' I answered, climbing to my feet and smoothing out my skirt.

'We might want to go on inside,' Clark said. 'It looks like rain.'

'I think it won't arrive until later tonight. We can use the rain,' I said, thinking of the corn and peas sprouting in the Victory Garden out in back of 'Two Trees'.

Clark walked me back to my building. He took my arm as we started up the stone steps. Again I detected no romantic spark between us. So odd that he sought out my company this way. The thought that he was vetting me for some kind of promotion or mission at OSS crossed my mind again. I hoped I was making the right impression. And thank God Sergeant Royal and I had ended our partnership without compromising me!

'Can you come out with me tonight?' Clark asked. 'Rose and I have someone we'd like you to meet. He's a friend of ours. The plan is to meet him at Rose's and then go out to eat somewhere. Sadie's working tonight, but Peggy might come.'

'I don't usually go out on a week night, Clark,' I said.

'We won't be out late. After dinner I'll take you home. And we'll leave early, directly from here, if that's OK. Our friend wants to meet you.'

On the off chance that Clark was testing me I decided I should say yes.

'Sure,' I said. 'Meet you on the usual corner.'

'Clark, you missed the turn,' I said.

'No I didn't.'

'You just passed Rose and Sadie's apartment building.'

'Oh,' he said, 'I must have misspoken. We're going to meet our friend at his place. He lives just a little way further along.'

My gut told me something suspicious was happening, and I should have listened to it. I really should have. We pulled up to the Worth Hotel, where Hughes/Anderson had rented his secret room.

'Here we are,' Clark said, parking across the street. 'I know it's not impressive but our friend is rarely home and you know how tough it is to find housing in the District.'

I collected my things but Clark put a hand on my arm. 'We need to wait a few minutes. We come separately so as not to pique the curiosity of that awful female custodian. Peggy should already be inside.' He checked his watch.

Then I saw Rose walking quickly down the sidewalk, her head bent to avoid the rain. She paused at the entrance to the hotel and checked her watch before going on inside.

'Just a few minutes,' Clark said to me.

Only an idiot would still think this was a social occasion! What was going on?

As Clark opened my door for me and handed me out I resisted the urge to tear my hand out of his and run wildly down the street screaming for the police. I didn't know what was about to happen but I was sure I wasn't going to like it. If Clark was taking me to Hughes' room, then he must know that Hughes had a second identity, and if so perhaps he had something to do with Hughes' murder. Unfortunately running away was not an option. After all I did work for OSS and I had to find out what was going on.

'Thanks, Clark,' I said, taking my hand from his as I stepped on to the sidewalk. I wanted to be free to bolt if I needed to. Inside the hotel the custodian's window was closed, thank God, so she couldn't recognize me. Clark and I walked up to the second floor and turned down the hall until we got to room 2G, Hughes' room that he had rented under the name of Anderson. The door was ajar. Inside Rose was laying out a few clothes and personal belongings on the bed. An open suitcase stood nearby. Peggy stood watch at the only window, her hands stuffed into the pockets of a trench coat. She must be expecting rain too.

'Hi, Louise!' Rose said, and came over to hug me. 'Are you surprised?'

'Yes,' I said, my voice cracking. I coughed to cover up my nervousness. 'Where are we?'

'This is a safe room,' Clark said. 'Paul Hughes rented it for us.'

'I'm packing up the things he kept here,' Rose said. She loaded the suitcase quickly with the few items on the bed. Among them I noted a key ring that held three keys, a pocketknife and a cigarette lighter. Items that should have been in Hughes' pocket when his corpse was discovered! I felt myself hold my breath while I looked for a wallet, but I didn't see one. Did Hughes leave this room with just his wallet the night he died?

'We'll need to find a new safe room now,' Rose said.

'What for?' I asked, dreading the answer.

'Have a seat,' Clark said. 'Let us explain.'

I sat on the bed but kept my feet on the ground. I still wanted to be able to bolt. I recalled that there were three exits from the hotel – the front door, the back door and the fire escape, so conveniently located off the end of the hall not far from the door to this room.

'Don't look so worried, Louise,' Rose said, sitting down next to me. 'We're your friends.'

'Louise, in your work you must see all kinds of useful intelligence pass across your desk,' Clark said. 'Much of it would be of interest to our friends in the Soviet Union.'

Oh my God!

'You know the Soviet Union is our ally,' Clark continued, 'yet so much is kept from them, despite the critical value of the Second Front. As you know there's not a single Soviet representative at the Trident Conference.'

Oh my God. They – Clark, Rosie, Paul Hughes, and Sadie and Peggy too – were double agents! Spying for the Soviet Union! And they were trying to recruit me! Now I understood why Clark spent so much time with lowly government girls. They were his agents!

Clark was standing between me and the door, and he was a big man.

'It's easy,' Rose said. 'And we're so very careful.'

'I'll give you an example of what the NKVD wants to know,' Clark said. 'During the Trident Conference today, when I was taking notes for Dr Soong, an American delegate reported that at current production levels it would be impossible for the US to produce the eight thousand five hundred landing craft that would be needed in an invasion of France by next spring. Don't you think our allies should know that? Shouldn't the Soviet Union know that the United States and Great Britain might not make the timetable of a spring invasion? How many more Russian soldiers might die on the Second Front then?'

I found my voice. 'Shouldn't the President and Director Donovan make the decision on what to share with the Soviet Union?' I asked.

'Why is there a Chinese representative at the Trident Conference and not a Soviet one? The Joint Chiefs, the British Field Marshals, Churchill and Roosevelt, they are all making decisions without the Soviets, damn it!' Clark's voice rose. His fists clenched and unclenched as he spoke. 'Do you know why the Soviets are left out in the cold?' he continued. 'Western allied leaders are afraid of the Soviet Union. Of the new kind of democracy being born there. One where the people are really in charge. Not oligarchs who have no interest in the ordinary man or woman, except to have them work in their factories and fight in their wars. Roosevelt, Churchill, even de Gaulle are terrified that a socialist revolution will follow the war in their own countries.'

'I don't know about this,' I said, stalling for time while I tried to decide what to do. What would happen to me if I refused? I found it hard to believe that Clark or Rose would harm me. But someone killed Paul Hughes!

'Louise, it's so, so exciting to be a part of something this important!' Rose said. 'To help our Communist friends! You are a Communist, aren't you?'

They had mistaken my progressive notions for Communism.

'No,' I said. 'I am not. I'm a New Dealer.'

'It's all right to hesitate to admit your allegiances,' Clark said. 'Especially where we work, and at your level. I understand. Let me introduce you to someone who will calm all your fears.'

Clark opened the door to the hall and a man stepped into the room. He was the stooped elderly Russian who owned the news and sundries shop. He didn't look stooped and elderly now. With his modest suit and grey hair combed neatly behind his ears he could have passed as an insurance salesman until he spoke.

'Louise Pearlie, let me introduce you to our colleague, Lev Gachev,' Clark said.

'G'! I had finally met 'G'!

'Mrs Pearlie knows me as Lieb Zruchat,' Gachev said. 'We met last week at my store. Apparently someone pretending to be Paul's mother sent a telegram using my return address. Mrs Pearlie's cover was very convincing. If I hadn't spotted her when she left Rose and Sadie's apartment after their last social evening she would have convinced me completely.'

Rose and Clark both stared at us. 'You've met Lev?' Rose asked.

'Who sent the telegram?' Clark asked.

Gachev sat down on the bed next to Rose, who had finished packing Hughes' things and set the suitcase on the floor. Peggy still leaned up against the window sill, her eyes fixed on the street outside. She hadn't said a word yet.

Gachev shook a finger at Rose and Clark. 'What errands she has been running for OSS may matter nothing, depending on her answer to our request for her help.' He turned to me. 'May I call you Louise?' Gachev said.

'Yes.' Can I call you spymaster? I wondered how many rings Gachev operated.

'Let me assure you how safe your association with us would be,' Gachev said. 'We require nothing written from you. No notes, no documents removed from your office, no copies, nothing. You and I would meet alone, sometimes in my store where maybe you would stop by to buy another Baby Ruth. Sometimes in a safe room, like this one. You would tell me what intelligence you think our friends in the Soviet Union would be interested in knowing. In my cables to the NKVD I would assign you a code name that no one would know but me. There would be no evidence against you at all. And, of course, you must tell us everything you know about Paul Hughes' murder.'

Peggy clapped both hands over her mouth to keep from crying out.

'Yes, my dear,' Gachev said, turning to her, 'Paul was murdered. I don't know by whom.'

Clark was speechless, staring at me as if he couldn't believe I knew more about Hughes' death than he did.

'What if I join your little spy ring and you're arrested?' I said.

'My dear,' he said, 'I fought for the Bolsheviks during the Revolution. At one point I spent some months in the custody of the czar's interrogators. They got nothing from me. In the end I became so thin I was able to squeeze between my cell wall and the iron bars of the cell and escape. Nothing you Americans could do to me could force me to talk.'

I wondered where his radio transmitter was located. Maybe at the Soviet Embassy?

'I don't know,' I answered him. 'I'd have to think about it.'

Clark was nervous, flexing and relaxing his fists over and over again. 'Louise! I don't understand what you have to think about!' he said.

'You agreed with us about everything we talked about!' Rose said. 'And at the restaurant you backed up those black girls with us!'

'None of the opinions I expressed were any different from Eleanor Roosevelt's. Why don't you go ask her to spy for you?'

Peggy, one hand still covering her mouth, turned back to her post at the window.

'This is a very dangerous situation,' Gachev said to Clark, shoving his hands into his pockets where I was quite sure he gripped a gun. 'She could report us. Me, I could take refuge in the Soviet Embassy. What would happen to you three?'

Rose stood up from the bed, her face pale as a ghost. 'Louise,' she said, 'you wouldn't!'

'Of course not,' I said, lying with a straight face. I turned to Gachev. 'I don't want anything to happen to my friends here. I'll make a deal with you. You let me go, and I won't say anything to OSS Security. But you all,' and I caught Clark's eyes, 'must stop spying for the Soviet Union. Now.'

'That sounds fair,' Rose said, eagerly turning to Gachev, her eyes pleading with him.

'Clark,' Gachev said, ignoring Rose. 'It is up to you to convince Mrs Pearlie to cooperate with us.'

'I will, absolutely. I'm sure I can convince her.'

'You have twelve hours,' he said.

Or what? I thought. I'd wind up floating face down in the Tidal Basin like Paul Hughes? Had Hughes changed his mind about spying for the Soviet Union? Was that what his Sunday meeting with 'G' – Gachev – was about?

'This is what we are going to do,' Gachev said. 'Peggy, you take Paul's suitcase down the front stairs and leave through the main entrance. Make sure that scraggly woman sees you. On your way home dump the case into a garbage bin.'

Peggy still hadn't spoken. She tied her trench coat belt, then reached into a coat pocket and pulled out a scarf splotched with yellow flowers. My God, she had been Paul's lover! That explained her inappropriate grief after his death. I wondered if the others knew. Peggy lifted the suitcase and left.

'Rose, in five minutes you leave by the side door,' Gachev said.

Before Rose left she turned to me. 'Louise, please!'

I had to drop my eyes from her face, she looked so terrified.

'I will take my usual path down the fire escape,' Gachev said. 'Mrs Pearlie, remember, twelve hours.'

The door closed and we could hear the window in the hall open, then shut, as Gachev climbed out and started down the fire escape.

'Clark,' I began.

'Don't say it, Louise, I'm so sorry. I misjudged you. You seemed to agree with so much we talked about.'

'I thought Rose just wanted to be my friend. I thought you might be vetting me for a new OSS job,' I said. 'Instead you were trying to convince me to become a traitor.'

'We're not traitors!' Clark said. 'The Soviet Union is our ally! The Soviet people need us, God knows the NKVD is not getting the intelligence it needs from the allies.'

I looked him straight in the eye. 'Under no conditions am I going to cooperate with Gachev,' I said. 'I'd rather die first.'

'Jesus,' Clark said. He sank down on the bed. 'What am I going to do?'

'We must go to the OSS Security Office and tell Major Wicker everything.'

'No,' he said. 'I'd be ruined. Rose and Sadie's lives would be ruined. And Peggy and Spencer's. It's unthinkable! There must be another answer.'

'Was Spencer a part of this?'

'No, he has no idea. Peggy and Paul had an affair. Spencer was always working. Paul convinced Peggy to memorize parts of the strategic memos she typed and pass them on to him.'

I edged toward the door. I could kick off my shoes and take off. Once I got out into the street I would be safe.

Clark smiled at me like a child distracting me before he stole my candy. He pulled a derringer out of his jacket pocket. 'I have no desire to hurt you,' Clark said, 'but I will if I need to. I need time to think.'

'I suppose Gachev killed Paul Hughes. Did Hughes change his mind about cooperating?' I asked.

Clark shook his head. 'If Gachev had killed Paul he would have done a better job of it. Shot him between the eyes and hidden his body where it would never be found. Not floating in the Tidal Basin right out in the open.'

'Then who sent the telegram?' I asked.

Clark's hands shook. I could see the derringer barrel quiver.

'I have no idea,' he said.

'Rethink this, Clark,' I said. 'Let's go to OSS. It's inevitable. Security can keep you all safe.'

'Shut up,' he said, in a harsh voice I hadn't heard before. 'Put on your coat.'

'Where are we going?'

'I'm going to stash you somewhere you'll be safe for the twelve hours I need to figure our way out of this.'

My heart started to pound.

'Don't mistake me, Louise. I don't want to hurt you. I don't want Gachev to hurt you or Rose or Sadie. But I am not going to be revealed as a double agent and have my life ruined. You do as I say or I can't protect you.' He tossed me my raincoat.

'Button up,' he said. 'The weather is turning.'

SEVEN

Be tactful in issuing instructions or in making criticisms.
Women are often sensitive; they can't shrug off harsh
words in the way that men do. *Never* ridicule a woman—
it breaks her spirit and cuts off her efficiency.
'1943 Guide to Hiring Women', *Mass Transportation*
magazine, July 1943.

C lark gripped my arm tightly above the elbow and
shoved me out of Hughes' room. His right hand went
back into his pocket, where he no doubt retained a
firm grip on the derringer.

'Let's go,' he said.

The custodian's window was open but I couldn't see her,
though I could hear her radio playing distantly.

Outside the sky was dark and the wind had picked up. Trash
skittered along the sidewalk. The wind lifted my hair, but I
had nothing to tie it back with.

Clark urged me along the sidewalk. Instead of going to his
car we walked around the corner and two blocks north. We
came to an informal taxi stand, a café with four cabs parked
out front. The drivers were drinking coffee inside.

Clark opened the door and lifted his hand and one of the
drivers nodded, draining his coffee cup and meeting us at his
taxi. Clark beat him to the rear door and opened it for me,
scooting me along the back seat as he joined me. The cabbie
started his cab and flipped the meter.

'Where to?' he asked.

'Maine and "O",' Clark said.

'You sure you want to go down to the water?' the cabbie
asked. 'There's a big storm coming.'

'We need to check on our boat, don't we, honey?' Clark said, squeezing my arm.

'Yes, yes we do,' I said.

Maine and 'O' was a damn long way away, many blocks, almost to the mouth of the Washington Channel. I did not miss the irony of passing the Tidal Basin on our way. When we went under the railroad bridge, where the Pennsylvania RR tracks crossed the Potomac, we kept driving past the Municipal Fish Wharf, the Capital Yacht Club, the Norfolk and Washington Steamboat Line, the Harbor Police and the Potomac River Line. Along the way I saw boat owners tying down deck furniture and toting gear down to their boats' cabins. Most of the boats flew American flags of various sizes; they all fluttered furiously in the wind. Raindrops began to spatter the taxi windshield.

When the taxi dropped us off the fare was about half of my monthly salary, which Clark paid in cash without batting an eye. I wondered if Gachev paid Clark for his espionage.

'Come on,' Clark said, pulling me down a wharf that extended out into the Washington Channel. We stopped at a small wooden runabout rolling in the swell. 'Get in,' he said.

'Clark,' I said. 'Please don't!' I thought he might be planning to take me out to the middle of the Potomac River and drown me.

'Be quiet,' he said, climbing down beside me and tossing off the mooring line. 'I'm trying to save your life. And mine too, for that matter. I'm putting you somewhere safe, where no one will find you, until I figure out just how to handle this.'

Clark pushed off from the dock while I crouched in the rear of the runabout. It had no awning, so soon my hair dripped from the soft steady rain. Clark reached past me to crank up the inboard motor and we slowly turned and made our way south and west, out of the Washington Channel and into the Potomac River. It was slow going. Since the war began the Potomac had become a parking lot for all kinds of vessels. Navy and coast-guard ships were anchored everywhere, but also sailboats, motor launches, yachts, anything that floated where someone could live. The housing shortage in the District was that tight. We had to creep around until we reached open water where the larger yachts were moored. Then we motored further west until I could see lights on the Virginia shore.

I had no idea where we were, except we had passed under no bridges, which meant that we must be south of the railway bridge.

We drew alongside a small sailboat moored in the sheltering arm of a short peninsula off the Virginia coast somewhere. There were several other boats moored nearby, but not nearly as many as clustered on the District side. They all seemed unoccupied. Clark cut the motor and tossed a rope over one of the sailboat's cleats and pulled the two boats together.

'Get into the sailboat,' he said. I complied and he followed me, lashing the two vessels together. The sailboat itself was tiny. The deck was just large enough to hold four people seated on the two wooden benches, one on each side. The small sail was neatly furled and the boom secured. A hatch sealed with a heavy padlock led to below decks.

I knew what Clark intended to do.

'Don't, Clark, please,' I said. 'Don't leave me down there!'

'You'll be perfectly safe,' he said, drawing a key from an inside pocket. 'There's a lantern and some tinned food.'

'So,' I said. 'This is your solution to your problem? Leave me here to die?'

'You stupid girl,' he said. 'I'm hiding you where no one can find you until I figure out a way out of this mess. No one I have ever tried to recruit has turned me down. Why didn't you agree, at least until Gachev was gone? I've not seen him look like that before. Brutal.'

He was right. I'd made another stupid mistake. I should have agreed to join the spy ring, then turned Leach in to Wicker as soon as possible. Instead I was so irate I refused his offer and found myself in another dangerous mess.

Clark unlocked the padlock and opened the hatch to the cabin and, grasping my arm, shoved me inside. There were only four wooden steps down, but I stumbled and fell, hoping

I could take Clark off guard. No luck. He jumped down from the ladder and hauled me to my feet. The cabin was so small we could barely stand upright together.

Clark gestured to the only bunk. 'Sit,' he said. 'I'll be on my way.'

I tried again to stall him. 'How did you even meet Gachev?' I asked.

'At a Communist Party of America dinner. Don't look at me like that. The CPUSA is a legal organization. General Secretary Browder spoke. Gachev and I were at the same table and we became friends. Later he asked me to help funnel useful intelligence to the NKVD. I was happy to do it. I still believe in the cause,' he said, staring me down. 'The current world political and economic system won't survive the war. So I recruited Paul and Rose. Rose brought in Sadie and Paul brought in Peggy.'

'Not Spencer.'

'No. Spencer is a capitalist through and through. When Rose met you she thought you were a possibility.' Because I believed in the same things Eleanor Roosevelt did – desegregation, women's rights and the labor movement – this amateur spy thought I was traitor material. Good God.

A vicious lightning bolt, visible through the port light, cracked through the sky, then lit up the night. Thunder rumbled and the boat's gentle rocking motion grew more agitated.

Heavy raindrops spattered on the boat deck, sounding loudest on the hatch door.

'There's a thunderstorm coming, Clark!' I said. 'I could die here!'

'Don't be foolish. It's just another spring storm. This boat has been moored here for two years. You'll be fine.'

Clark turned and climbed up the ladder to the deck, closing the hatch behind him. He turned the key in the heavy padlock and I heard the lock engage.

I pulled myself up the short ladder and screamed at him through the hatch. 'Liar! Traitor! You're not coming back to get me! You know I'll turn you in to OSS Security! You're

leaving me here to die! I've got a pen in my purse!' I
screamed. 'I'll write down everything! All over my body if
I have to! When they find me it'll all be there! They'll hang
you!'

'Louise,' Clark shouted at me, 'Don't be so melodramatic!
I'll be back for you! I just need time to think!'

Shortly I heard the runabout's engine engage and the boat
pull away. Leaving me in the dim sailboat cabin alone.

The cabin was bigger than a coffin and smaller than the
bathroom I shared at 'Two Trees' with Ada and Phoebe. I
felt panic rise for a minute, shivering fear coursing through
my body, as I wondered if I would ever see 'Two Trees'
again. Or my parents, whom I hadn't written in a month.
Or Joe! To think I'd hesitated to visit him! What a little fool
I'd been.

I suppose it was possible that Clark did intend to come back
for me, but I wasn't going to count on it. So I explored my
diminutive prison for supplies and maybe a potential escape
route.

First I smacked my head on a kerosene lantern swaying
overhead. I heard liquid sloshing and found matches in the
only drawer in the cabin, one next to the tiny two-burner
propane stove. The flame rose in the lamp and cast its light
over the warm wood that paneled the cabin and instantly I felt
more hopeful. There was something about the light that was
reassuring. In contrast there was very little light coming in
now through the two narrow port lights, one on each side of
the cabin. Even if they hadn't been rusted shut only a cat could
have got through them.

The only bunk stretched along one side of the cabin.
Opposite it was the tiny galley with a sink and the stove. A
shelf that held a few cans of beans and soup and a jar of
instant coffee restrained by a rope ran along the cabin wall
over the stove. Thank God for the coffee.

A narrow door at the rear of the cabin opened into the head.
The toilet hadn't been pumped out recently but I had smelled
worse. And there was toilet paper.

If I was convinced that Clark was returning to me the facilities were bearable for a couple of days. But I was not convinced.

I noticed one encouraging prop. A life preserver hung on the wall next to the door to the deck. So, I thought optimistically, if I could get out of here I could paddle to Virginia safely. But not during a storm. I would need to wait until it passed. And I had no clue how to get out of the cabin with the hatch closed so securely. I edged myself as far back in the cabin as I could. The rear hatch, which opened so a winch could raise the sail, was locked from the outside too. It was too small for me to climb through anyway.

A giant crack of thunder made me jump while a lightning strike coursed across the bit of sky I could see through the port light. Wow, I thought, that wasn't far away. The boat's rocking intensified. I hoped I didn't get seasick. That was all I needed.

The trapdoor to the hold took up much of the cabin floor. I grasped the ring handle and pulled the door up easily. Holding the lantern over the dark opening, I saw what seemed to me to be a normal amount of water sloshing around. Closing the hold I hung the lantern on its ring on the ceiling again. The light swayed as the boat rocked, more than it had just a few minutes earlier.

I wasn't afraid of the water. I was born and raised on the coast of North Carolina and had been in so many boats, sometimes in stormy weather, that I couldn't count them. And I swam like a fish. What concerned me, what terrified me, was the prospect that this little sailboat couldn't withstand this storm, and that locked below I wouldn't have a chance to escape.

I forced myself to be calm, reassuring myself that Clark was right. This boat had weathered many a tempest right here in this anchorage. It would be unpleasant to be locked down here during a thunderstorm, but after it was over maybe I could think of a way out.

*   *   *

Royal stared down at Clark Leach's corpse. It lay face up, eyes wide open, legs tangled around a chair that had toppled over when he fell. The bullet had entered his skull precisely between his eyes. Whoever had executed him had done this before.

The deceased was easily identified by his driver's license and an OSS identification tag. The thought that the dead man was OSS, like Paul Hughes, made Royal feel tired.

The woman who owned the little café, just four tables in the main room of her row house, waited in the kitchen with a policewoman. Rain pummeled the metal roof of the house and a flash of lightning lit the dim room briefly.

'I do not need to have restaurant license,' she said to Royal immediately. 'Small. Only four tables. I cook for homesick Russians.'

'Ma'am,' Royal said. 'I am not interested in your business. I just want to know what happened here. Now, what is your name?'

The woman was not young but still handsome, her dark hair bundled on top of her head and covered with a knitted cap. She had a good, if matronly, figure under her spotless apron. Her grey eyes hadn't left his face yet. She wasn't afraid, she simply didn't want to give Royal her name. She came from a place where the police were thugs.

'You must, you know,' the policewoman said to her.

'My name is Ekaterina Korobkina,' she said. 'May I have a cigarette?'

'Of course,' Royal said. 'Would you like one of mine?'

'No thank you,' she said. 'I smoke Sobranie.' She pulled a single cigarette wrapped in black paper out of her apron pocket. Royal offered her a light and she accepted it.

'You're Russian,' Royal said.

'Yes,' she said. 'My husband and I emigrate to America in 1937, from Novgorod.'

'Where is your husband?'

'At work. He has a night shift.'

'Please tell me what happened.'

'Two men came in to eat. The one that is dead and another. They ordered *pirozkhi*. While I am cooking I hear them arguing. Then a gunshot. I call the police. I hide in the pantry with a stool shoved under the doorknob until I hear police siren. That is all.'

'Did you know the men?'

'No I did not,' she said. 'I have never seen them before.'

'Mrs Korobkina,' Royal said. 'The dead man isn't Russian. You cook Russian food for exiled Russians. I will bet you my pension that the other man, the murderer, is Russian and that he has been here before. What is his name?'

She shrugged, crossing her arms. 'I do not know him,' she said. Royal didn't interrogate her further. He could tell from her expression that she'd rather go to an American jail than reveal the man's name.

The crime team arrived, a photographer and a fingerprint expert. The morgue wagon parked at the curb, waiting to receive the body. Royal directed the policewoman to sit with Mrs Korobkina until her husband came home from work. He left the constable who had answered the original call with him to keep everyone except Mrs Korobkina's husband out of the house. Then he dashed across the street in the rain to wait in his police car so he could take some weight off his bad knee. Once inside he stretched across the front seat and lit his own cigarette.

A Buick sedan with government plates drew up in front of him. A broad man in an Army uniform got out of the car.

Damn it, Royal thought, the Army! He should have realized the military would intrude, with Russians and the OSS involved. This would be yet another case where the Feds would tell him to go find lost dogs instead of solving a cold-blooded murder.

The man ran over to Royal's car and knocked on his window. Royal rolled it down, letting the man stand in the rain.

'I'm Major Angus Wicker, OSS Security,' the man said.

Flip you a dead fish, Royal thought. He dropped his cigarette and shook hands with Wicker. 'Sergeant Harvey Royal, District Police, homicide.'

'Can we talk?'

'If we must.'

Wicker went around the car and slid into the passenger seat, after Royal drew his legs back under the steering wheel.

'I know the deceased is Clark Leach,' Wicker said. 'One of ours. The chief of police telephoned us after you called it in. Do you know who shot him?'

Royal shook his head. 'No. The woman runs a small café out of her house cooking for the Russian émigré community. She refused to identify the Russian man our victim was eating dinner with. Don't think we'll be able to get her to, either.'

'Wise woman,' Wicker said. 'She doesn't want to get mixed up in whatever is going on.'

Royal wanted to go home and have a couple of stiff bourbons to ease the pain in his knee. But he needed to ask the question.

'Don't suppose you'd be willing to help us out here, would you?' he asked Wicker.

Wicker stared across the street at the Korobkina house.

'Can I go inside? See the body?' Wicker asked.

'Sure. Why not?'

The two men hurried across the street and into the front room of the house. The police photographer was picking up the light bulbs he'd ejected while photographing the body. The fingerprint expert was packing all his little bottles and brushes into a leather case. Wicker stood over the corpse and stared at him.

'Let's go back outside,' Wicker said, abruptly turning away from the dead man. 'Better yet, let's get a drink. We can take my car.'

'Constable,' Royal said to the policeman. 'When the crime scene guys are finished you may release the body to the morgue. Ask if you can help Mrs Korobkina in any way. The policewoman will stay with her until her husband arrives home. Then you may release the scene and leave.'

'Yes sir,' the policeman said.

*   *   *

Wicker and Royal ran, their trench coats pulled over their heads to protect them from the rain, into a brightly lit pub. The barman gestured them toward the bar, but Royal flashed his badge and he and Wicker took the only empty booth. Both men ordered double bourbons.

'Clark Leach was a big shot,' Wicker said, after their bourbons arrived. 'Far East specialist. Close to General Donovan.'

'Oh my God,' Royal said. 'You don't happen to know who killed him?'

'Pretty sure it was Lev Gachev, Russian émigré, a spymaster for the Soviet Union. Runs a couple of small spy rings inside the government. He turned Leach.'

When Royal recovered from his astonishment at Wicker's confidences he suggested that the District Police could put out an All Points Bulletin on Gachev.

'No, he's long gone. Abandoned his cover – a little shop, I just came from there. He's either tucked up at the Soviet Embassy or in another safe house.'

'So is that it?' Royal asked. 'You guys are planning to cover this up too, I suppose.'

Wicker paused, staring at Royal as if sizing him up, then said 'We believe Gachev murdered Paul Hughes too. Hughes was a member of the same ring that Leach ran. We think that Hughes had just met with Gachev. They must have had a disagreement. The Tidal Basin is just a few blocks from what was Gachev's shop.'

'Sounds reasonable.'

Royal gestured the bartender for another double bourbon. Wicker declined with a shake of his head.

'Who sent the telegram from Hughes' "mother"?' Royal said, sipping instead of gulping his second drink.

'We assume Gachev,' Wicker said. 'His shop's address was recorded at the local Western Union office. Incredible he would make such an error.'

'So both cases are solved,' Royal said. Louise would be glad to know this, he thought.

He hoped her job was safe.

'Not exactly. We have a very loose end to tie up,' Wicker said.

'What?' Royal asked.

'Do you know the whereabouts of Mrs Louise Pearlie? We've lost track of her.'

EIGHT

Get enough size variations in [. . .] uniforms that each girl can have a proper fit. This point can't be stressed too strongly as a means of keeping women happy.
'1943 Guide to Hiring Women', *Mass Transportation* magazine, July 1943.

Royal sipped his bourbon to buy a few seconds to think. 'Louise who?' he asked.

'Louise Pearlie,' Wicker said. 'You don't need to dissemble. We know you've met with her regarding the Hughes murder.'

'Yes,' Royal said. He sucked on his cigarette again, stalling, not knowing what to tell Wicker. He'd promised not to inform on Louise to OSS, but he didn't know what to make of this situation.

'Let me begin,' Wicker said. 'Mrs Pearlie is a file clerk, but she's done some commendable fieldwork in the past, so we asked for her help in resolving some small issues in the Hughes case. Apparently you approached her too?'

'Yes,' Royal said, giving in to his concern about Louise. 'She gave her real name to Hughes' landlady, Mrs Nighy. Once you people put the kibosh on my investigation of Hughes' murder, I used her mistake to get her to work for me. You see, my superiors had closed the Hughes' case, but I was sure he was murdered.'

'She investigated for us at the same time,' Wicker said. 'Playing both ends against the middle. She's a smart woman.'

'Mrs Pearlie never told me anything I couldn't have found out myself if I'd been authorized to investigate the case.'

'Forget about all that,' Wicker said. 'We have more than that to worry about. The last time Mrs Pearlie was seen she was with Clark Leach.'

'No!' Royal said. He felt his throat constrict.

Wicker leaned forward. 'This is complicated, so I'm just going to hit the high spots. While all this commotion over the Hughes murder was going on, a woman at OSS approached Mrs Pearlie, under the guise of offering her friendship. She introduced her to a group of friends, including Clark Leach. Paul Hughes was a member of the circle before he died. Another friend is the wife of yet another big shot at OSS. The group met every week for drinks at the apartment of two of the women. They went out to a nightclub. Leach took Mrs Pearlie to a movie.'

'How did you know this?'

'We've suspected Leach for some time. We've had a tail on him for weeks. Mrs Pearlie has a sterling record so we allowed the ring's attempt to recruit her to continue.'

'I don't suppose you had the grace to tell her.'

'No, strategically we felt the operation would work better if she wasn't briefed.'

'And all this intertwines with the Hughes murder?' Royal asked.

'Yes. Figuring it all out is like trying to untie a fisherman's knot with one hand,' Wicker said.

Royal put his hands flat on the table and pushed hard to relieve the tension in his back and neck.

'If Louise is in danger we're wasting time! When were she and Leach last seen?' he asked.

'Leaving a residential hotel near Hughes' rooming house a couple of hours ago,' Wicker said. 'We think the ring kept a safe room there. Louise and Leach arrived together, our man on Leach's tail. Two of the women arrived separately earlier. And our man saw Gachev enter through a side door a minute after Leach and Louise went in the main entrance. I think this is when the group tried to recruit Louise. Later they all came out separately, except for Louise and Leach. The two of them left together, and our man said Leach was gripping Louise's arm in an unfriendly way, you might say.'

'So where did they go!'

'Our man lost them. Instead of using Leach's car the two of them went around the corner and up a couple of blocks to a taxi stand. Our man ran after them and arrived at the taxi stand just as their taxi drove off.'

'License plate?'

'No. And a couple of hours later Leach is murdered.'

'Damn!' Royal exploded. 'We've got to do something!'

'I'm afraid to hope she might still be alive.'

'We need to assume she is. Do you know these girls who made friends with Louise?'

'Yes, but I can't tell you their names.'

'For Christ's sake! You and your goddamn secrecy! Look, find the girls, ask them if they can think of any place that Leach might have taken Louise. Beat it out of them with a chair if you have to!'

'What about you?' Wicker said, standing up.

'I'm familiar with that taxi cab stand. I'm going to find the driver who picked up Louise and Leach. Take me back to my car; let's go!'

'How can we keep in touch?'

'Do you have a radio in your car?'

'Yeah.'

'I'll give you the police frequency.'

The tiny sailboat tossed violently, straining its anchor line like a leashed dog trying to chase a squirrel. I'd already tied myself to a rung of the ladder steps to keep from being thrown around the cabin. Now I heaved. My head pounded. Although I'd spent a lot of time around boats, the wood creaking, the grating sound that the anchor rope made in its socket and the cracks of lightning that lit up the square of sky that showed in the portholes terrified me. I tried to calm myself as best I could. I wouldn't be any safer above deck, would I? I'd have to tie myself to the main mast to keep from being tossed overboard and I'd be sopping wet to boot. That was all well and good, but I was locked below deck. If the ship was damaged I'd have no chance at all of living. I'd go right down with it. Fear took total hold of me for a few minutes. I screamed wildly and I felt urine dribble down my legs. I had such a bad headache from the low barometer I thought my skull would split open.

One of the port lights went mystifyingly dark. How I regained control of myself I don't remember. But I untied myself and struggled over to the port light and peered out into the night.

Clouds cleared, briefly revealing the moon, and in its light I saw the enormous anvil shape of the storm, lightning threading through it, looming over me.

This was a damn big storm. It could spawn a waterspout.

I made my way to the head, but not before being thrown up against the stove, so hard it left my left arm almost numb. Inside the head I relieved myself, heaving into the tiny sink at the same time. I felt safer inside the head than out in the cabin, so there I stayed as I took mental inventory of the tiny cabin. For the life of me I could not imagine any possible way I could escape.

Thunder boomed almost directly overhead, or so it seemed, and I could feel the ship shudder, trying desperately to pull free from its anchor, almost bucking. I opened the door to the head in time to see a glimpse through a port light of a wave rearing up and pouring over the boat, which tilted sharply before righting itself.

I wished I hadn't stopped going to church. I wondered if it would count against me. After all, I'd gone to the Baptist church three days a week until moving to Washington, more than even the Catholics in Wilmington. For some reason the Navy hymn came to mind and I began to hum it to myself as loudly as I could. Its staid melody calmed me and helped me to feel hopeful. If God listened to the prayers of 'those in peril on the sea', surely I qualified!

Major Wicker pulled up in front of Rose and Sadie's apartment house.

'What is this?' he said to his driver, looking out the window at the raging storm outside. 'The end of days?'

Hail pummeled the sidewalk. When Wicker exited his car the wind almost knocked him down. He held on tight to his hat as he ran for the apartment house, icy ping-pong ball sized hail falling from the sky.

'God damn,' Wicker said to himself, once inside the lobby. 'This is all we need.'

He removed his hat and raincoat and headed to the elevator.

'So,' he said to the Army private who guarded Rose's door. 'How are they doing?'

'All I can hear is crying,' the constable said. 'And that WAAC girl trying to calm them down.'

'That WAAC's name is Private Godfrey,' Wicker said.

Inside on the sofa Rose and Sadie weren't crying anymore, but they were scrunched together on the sofa holding on to each other for dear life. The WAAC sat nearby, but stood to attention when Major Wicker came in the door.

'At ease,' Wicker said to Private Godfrey.

'Have you found Louise?' Rose asked. 'Is she all right?'

'What is going to happen to us?' Sadie asked. 'We are so sorry! We just didn't think!'

'We don't have time for that now.' He remained standing, a psychological ploy to make the women feel his authority and understand that time was short. 'We have not found Mrs Pearlie. She could be in terrible danger. We need your help.'

'Anything,' Rose said. 'We'll do anything!'

'When was the last time you saw Mrs Pearlie?' Wicker asked.

'When she left the safe room with Clark,' Rose said. 'After she refused to join our ring.'

'Under what circumstances?' Wicker asked.

The two women turned and looked at each other. Wicker saw from their eyes that agreement passed between them.

'Gachev gave Clark twelve hours to convince Louise to join us,' Rose said.

'It hasn't been twelve hours!' Sadie said. 'So Louise must still be alive!'

Wicker didn't mince words. 'Clark Leach is dead. Murdered

by Gachev in the middle of a café a couple of hours ago. Shot right between the eyes. Louise wasn't with them.'

Sadie made a wounded noise in her throat, then burst into tears. Rose shook her hard.

'Stop that!' Rose said. 'We both need to think straight!'

Sadie just cried harder, until she was almost shrieking. Wicker ordered Private Godfrey to take her into the bedroom and shut the door.

'Listen to me,' Wicker said to Rose, who was dry-eyed but trembling. 'Has Leach ever mentioned some place, other than his apartment, that he has access to, where he might have taken Louise while he dickered with Gachev? Someplace she couldn't escape from?'

'No,' Rose said. 'No. Nothing like that!'

'Think,' Wicker said. 'I'm not being dramatic when I say that Louise's life is at stake.'

Rose bit her lip and twisted her hands. Then a spark lit up her eyes. 'Clark told us about a little sailboat he could borrow that belonged to a friend. He said we could picnic there this summer. Sunbathe and listen to the radio.'

'Where?' Wicker said.

'It's moored on the Virginia side of the Potomac,' she said. 'South of the railroad bridge.'

God, Wicker thought. In this storm!

At first I thought I was dreaming. It seemed to me that the storm was abating. The rocking of the boat was less violent. Several times the line to the anchor slacked. Maybe the storm had passed through and I wasn't going to drown after all. I should have sung the Navy hymn to myself much earlier in this ordeal and included all the verses. Thunder still cracked and lightning flashed, but the thunder wasn't as loud and the lightning bolts struck further to the south. Perhaps I wasn't going to drown after all. I glanced at my watch. It was two o'clock in the morning, six hours since Clark had imprisoned me here, another six to go until he returned – if he returned. I was not counting on it.

I pushed my way out of the head and peered out one of the port lights. I hadn't been dreaming. It was still storming but the worst of it had passed on by.

The kerosene lantern had gone out, so I relit it. Its warm glow was so comforting it brought tears to my eyes. I lay down on the bunk and let tension ease out of my body.

After a few minutes' rest I got up and climbed the short ladder to the hatch door. I threw my shoulder into the door until it throbbed with pain, then switched to the other shoulder. The door didn't give even an inch, God damn it! In frustration I kicked the hatch hard, lost my balance and tumbled down the steps. If I lived through this I'd be covered with bruises.

Next I searched the cabin looking for something, anything, that might help me break through the door. Behind a compartment door I found a rivet gun. It was a heavy tool that looked like a wrench except for an added mechanism in the head that delivered the rivets.

Back at the hatch door I slammed the head of the rivet gun against the door over to the hasp screws as hard as I could, over and over. I scarred up the door, but that was all. If the padlock had been placed on the cabin side I might have been able to knock it loose, but from this side budging it was impossible. In frustration I flung the rivet gun across the length of the cabin. It bounced off the wall and landed on the propane stove with a clang.

Perhaps in the morning, when it was light, I would be able to think more clearly. I lay back down on the bunk and tried to rest.

A sound like a pine log dropping from a crane on to a truck bed woke me out of a thin sleep. I felt the boat tremble. It was an impact, a severe one. Something had struck the sailboat. I felt the cabin begin to list to one side. The ship was taking on water.

I jumped up and grasped the ring on the hatch to the hold and pulled it up. Holding the lantern over the square hole in the floor, I peered in and saw that without doubt the water was rising. I could hear the sound of water rushing into the hold but couldn't see the section of the hull where the damage was. My best guess was that the limb of a tree had rammed the ship right at the water line.

The ship was sinking.

Sergeant Royal pulled up to the taxi stand a couple of blocks away from the Worth Residential Hotel. He'd already found Leach's car still parked out in front of the hotel. Since Leach and Louise had left by taxi, Royal figured that Leach must have dropped her off somewhere, then taken another taxi to the Russian café to meet Gachev. Leach died before he could get back to his car.

The taxi cab stop was unofficial, with just a few cabs out in front of a small diner where the drivers could drink coffee and listen to baseball games on the radio while waiting for a fare. Royal parked out front, behind the row of taxis, and got out, sliding over slick lumps of hail on his way to the diner. He spotted the drivers right away crowded into a booth near the radio mounted on the back wall. He removed his badge from his pocket as he made his way over to the cab drivers. As soon as he got to their table he flashed it.

'DC Metropolitan Police,' Royal said. 'And I ain't got any time to waste.'

'What's this about, Sergeant?' one of the drivers asked.

'I'm doing the talking here, not you,' Royal said. 'I need to know who picked up a fare here about seven this evening. Middle-aged guy who looked like he might work for the government. Attractive woman in round-rimmed glasses and a raincoat, not young. They did not look like they were having fun.'

'It was me,' said one of the drivers, a scrawny guy with slicked back hair. 'The man had a hold of the woman's arm real tight and she didn't look pleased about it.'

'Where did you take them?' Royal asked.

'To the docks on the Washington Channel. Near the Capital Yacht Club. Hell of a drive from here. Nearly to the end of

Maine Avenue. One of the best fares I ever got. The guy paid me with a handful of cash as if it was nothing. Two dollars over the fare! And they just walked off.'

'Did you see where they went?'

'Down the wharf opposite the Capital Yacht Club. Damn rainy day to go on a boat ride.'

Royal drove with one hand on the wheel and the other gripping his radio mike. The radio static was bad because of the storm but he could still hear Wicker on the other end.

'The girls say that Leach had access to a little sailboat on the Potomac,' Wicker said. 'He talked about using it for a picnic. It's moored on the Virginia side below the railroad bridge.'

'That has to be it,' Royal said. 'I found the taxi driver who picked them up. He drove them all the way from the Worth Hotel to a wharf on the Washington Channel. Across from the Capital Yacht Club. He said that Leach gave him a handful of cash and took Louise down the wharf.'

'If Leach stowed Louise on that boat while he negotiated with Gachev she must still be there,' Wicker said.

'I'll meet you at the wharf,' Wicker said. 'We've got to find her. This is one hell of a storm to weather in a little sailboat.'

The coastguard captain of the port stood at the end of the wharf with Royal and Wicker. He'd lent the two men rubber raincoats and sou'westers. The storm had diminished but a heavy rain still fell steadily. Looking off the end of the wharf the men could see nothing but the shadows of boats moored a few feet from the end of the docks.

'I'm sorry,' said the coastguard captain, whose name was Meacham. 'I just can't institute a search tonight. Visibility is terrible. The electric current is out on the Virginia side so there's no loom to help us. No moon most of the time, either. And most of my cutters are guarding the entrance to the Potomac. The submarine net gates were left open because of the storm.'

'The woman we are searching for may be locked aboard a small sailboat,' Wicker said. 'It might have been damaged during the storm.'

'I can't risk my own men in these conditions,' Meacham said. 'I swear that as soon as daybreak comes I'll institute a full search. I'll call out the auxiliary too. We'll find her.'

'I hope it's not too late,' Royal said. If Louise was dead this would be the biggest failure of Royal's career. He'd retire with her death on his mind for the rest of his life.

Wicker knew that he'd made a terrible mistake by not briefing Louise on the true nature of Leach's ring, so that she could be on guard. He'd known from her personnel file that she was trustworthy and smart. He'd thought that she would react more naturally to events if she didn't know that she was being courted by a spy ring. He'd believed that Leach wasn't physically dangerous. It was only recently that OSS Security had identified Gachev. If Louise was dead he'd be the one who'd write her parents. What would he say? 'I'm responsible for the death of your daughter. So sorry.'

'It'll be a few hours until dawn,' Royal said. He needed a drink.

'We can wait at my HQ,' Meacham said. 'There's always a pot of coffee on. Or I've got something stronger in my desk.'

'Something stronger,' Wicker said.

So ironic. The storm was passing by, but I was still going to drown. And maybe never be found! Spending years lying on the bottom of the Potomac River hosting barnacles. Someday perhaps a fisherman would hook one of my bones and feel sorry for me after he reeled it in.

Growing up on the coast I knew lots of people who'd drowned. The Atlantic off North Carolina boasted nasty rip tides and powerful hurricanes. Then there were the folks who drank and surfed, or drank and sailed. And the occasional fisherman who got tangled up in his nets. Or the weekend sailor who was knocked overboard by his boom. But I'd never heard of anyone who drowned locked in the cabin of a sinking boat.

I sat on the bunk trying to quell the physical signs of my panic. Tears filled my eyes so I could barely see, my heart pumped so hard it resonated in my head, and my bladder and intestines contracted. I had no more ideas on how I could escape. Or fantasies, either. Only if Captain America showed up was I going to survive. If I only had a hand grenade!

A hand grenade! That was it!

Before I knew it I was at the galley rummaging in the cabinet under the stove looking for the propane bottle. I found it and unscrewed it from the line that fed the burners, quickly closing the shut-off valve. It was a small canister, about the size of a quart of milk. I hoped it had enough gas in it to do the trick. Not that this wild idea of mine was going to work, but I had to try it.

Opening a drawer I discovered a small miracle – duct tape! Duct tape was an adhesive tape that could hold absolutely anything together. It had been invented for military use but civilians could buy it now in hardware stores. It was just what I needed.

By now the boat listed to starboard at a significant angle. I almost had to crawl on the sloping floor to get to the hatch. With my arms wrapped around one of the side rails of the ladder to keep from falling, I taped the propane tank to the door. It wasn't easy to balance myself on the ladder, hang on to the propane tank, tear off sections of the duct tape, then tape the tank to the door, as near as possible to the screws that secured the hinged metal plate of the hasp to the door. On the other side of the door the heavy padlock held the loops of the hasp together. Would the blast be powerful enough to destroy the padlock without killing me too?

I gathered all my energy. I needed to accomplish a lot in the next few seconds. I twisted the valve on the propane canister and heard the hissing of gas escaping. Then I bolted toward the back of the cabin, grabbing the thin mattress from the bunk with one hand and lifting the kerosene lantern from its hook with the other. I backed up against the head.

Damn it! I forgot! I dropped the mattress and went back for the life ring. How could I hang on to all this stuff? How much propane had hissed away while I went back for the ring?

I backed up against the head again, with the life preserver hooked over my left arm, the mattress gripped in my left hand and the lantern in my right. I turned the lantern's control knob as high as possible. The flame leapt halfway up the globe.

I judged the distance between me and the propane tank as well as I could. Then I heaved the lantern directly at the tank and backed into the head, pulling the mattress and the life ring in after me.

It wasn't much of an explosion. Muffled up in the mattress as I was I barely heard it. The ship didn't react to the blast, if you could call it that, at all. There was no break to the slow rhythm of its sinking. There must not have been enough propane in the tank. I was devastated. Broken in spirit, I felt numb enough to be dead already. I thought about staying in the head so I couldn't see the water rise from the hold to engulf me, but instead I pushed away the mattress and went back into the cabin.

The hatch door was missing. Gone! Blown away!

I pulled the life ring over my head and entwined my arms in the ropes that circled it. I raced up the ladder through the gaping hole that had once been the hatch and flung myself on the deck. Sliding down the sloping deck I regained my footing by grasping the boat's handrail.

Gathering all my strength I climbed over the rail and leapt into the sea.

Rain was falling softly but I could see a few stars blinking in the night sky. What a beautiful, wonderful, stunning sight.

A loud gurgling noise distracted me from my admiration of the heavens. Kicking my legs, I swiveled to face the sailboat. It was sinking quickly now. The gurgle I'd heard was air bubbling up from the cabin. I watched the ship sink until the tip of the mast dipped under the ocean.

I was utterly exhausted. I leaned my head on to the ring and felt that I could fall asleep. But I shook myself awake.

I'd escaped drowning on the boat, but I could easily succumb to exhaustion and hypothermia if I didn't get out of the water. I could loose consciousness, slip right through the life ring and still drown. The District was too far away, all the way across the Potomac. I needed to paddle for the Virginia shore. There were no lights showing there, the electric current must be out, but I thought I could find my way if I could keep the stars in sight. And then clouds filled the sky again and I no longer knew where I was.

I was so tired I almost didn't care if I reached shore or not. Just as long as I wasn't trapped in that coffin of a ship's cabin anymore.

Then out of the wet silky mist a string of lights emerged.

NINE

[S]tress at the outset the importance of time—the fact that a minute or two lost here and there makes serious inroads on schedules. Until this point is gotten across, service is likely to be slowed up.

'1943 Guide to Hiring Women', *Mass Transportation* magazine, July 1943.

Three parallel strings of lights, actually. A motor yacht with three full decks came into view. With my last ounce of energy I screamed as loud as I could and kept screaming. The beam of a searchlight responded, streaming out from the yacht, roving across the water until it found me. Then I heard a bullhorn screech, and a voice cry out 'Man overboard!'

I was being rescued. I wanted to cry, but couldn't squeeze out any tears. I settled for a few moans instead.

A motor dinghy reached me quickly. I was hauled out of the water by two Navy seamen. One of them wrapped me in a heavy wool blanket while the other steered us back to the yacht.

Even in my exhausted state I could see that the yacht was lovely. All glowing wood and brass, every porthole streaming light, and a beautiful sun deck that stretched across the top of the second level, strewn about with deck chairs that looked like they belonged on a fancy cruise ship. A canvas roof stretched over the deck because of the storm.

My two rescuers half carried me up the yacht's ladder and when I reached the top two more Navy seamen helped me on board, exchanging my now soaked blanket for a new dry one.

I wondered why Navy sailors were manning a yacht.

I found out when I was escorted into the main salon and

met a middle-aged man, square in body and face, wearing round-rimmed spectacles. His thin hair was combed straight back from his forehead. He was wearing a silk dressing gown. I recognized him. He was Frank Knox, Secretary of the Navy. I was standing on the main deck of the *Sequoia*.

'Welcome aboard, ma'am,' Knox said. He stretched out a hand and I shook it. 'What on earth happened to you?' he asked.

I hesitated, tongue-tied. I had no idea what to say. I couldn't tell him the truth, could I?

Knox himself gave me an idea.

'Was this perhaps a personal incident, ma'am?'

'Yes, sir,' I answered. 'I went out on a party boat with some people I didn't know very well. Some of their activities were, well, unsavory. I became quite uncomfortable and wanted to get away from them. Had to get away, actually.'

I had just lied to a cabinet member.

'So you abandoned ship. Rather extreme, wasn't it?'

'Yes, sir. But I was in extreme circumstances.'

'There's no one else out there who needs rescuing, is there?'

'No, sir.'

'Good job, then, very good!' Knox said. 'All young ladies should take such good care of their reputations. Petty Officer Grymes,' Knox said.

'Yes, sir,' said the young sailor who'd been standing by my side, holding me up.

'Would you please show this young lady . . .' he began, then looked at me.

'Mrs Louise Pearlie,' I said.

'Would you please show Mrs Pearlie to one of the guest staterooms and see that she is comfortable? And try to find her something to wear.' Knox glanced at his watch. 'Dawn will break soon,' he said. 'Would you like to join me for an early breakfast at six?'

I was starving! 'Yes sir,' I said.

*   *   *

'Ma'am, there's a bathrobe and slippers in the closet,' Petty Officer Grymes said to me when he showed me into the tiny stateroom. 'And that door there leads to the bathroom. There's lots of hot water. If you'll toss your clothes outside your door we'll have them dried and ironed for you by the time we get into port. And I'll find something for you to wear in the meantime.'

'Thank you so much,' I said. 'When do you think we'll arrive?'

'I expect the captain will hoist anchor once the sun is fully up,' he said. 'We should dock at the Capital Yacht Club around eight in the morning.'

If Clark Leach did return to retrieve me from the boat it would be right about now and he would have quite a surprise waiting for him. Served him right.

When I joined Secretary Knox in the Grand Salon two places had been set at the long mahogany dining table that could easily seat twelve. The place settings gleamed with silver and china. I was wearing the uniform of a mess corpsman, white trousers and a white jacket that buttoned up to my neck, and the slippers I'd found in my stateroom closet. Knox had changed into a natty double-breasted suit that made him look even more box-like. The square of handkerchief tucked into his breast pocket matched his blue-striped tie.

'You look none the worse for wear,' Knox said to me, standing while a colored mess corpsman seated me.

'Thank you, Jim,' Knox continued, speaking to the corpsman. 'Mrs Pearlie, you are wearing Corpsman James Wood's spare mess uniform. You look much better in it than he does.'

'No one will argue with that, Mr Secretary,' Jim said.

'Thank you for lending me your clothes,' I said to the corpsman.

'You're welcome, ma'am,' he said as he poured my coffee. The odor of the coffee was overwhelmingly wonderful. I noticed there was plenty of sugar in Secretary Knox's sugar bowl. I shoveled three teaspoons into my cup.

As the sun rose over the Potomac the view outside the Grand Salon windows was breathtaking. What a wonderful place to live, I thought. I knew that Knox, who was separated from his wife, lived aboard the *Sequoia* full-time. It had been the President's yacht but Roosevelt had commissioned a bigger one for the duration of the war. The *Sequoia* had just four staterooms and the Grand Salon, not nearly enough for Roosevelt's entourage.

'I've ordered orange juice, waffles, eggs and bacon for breakfast,' Knox said. 'You're not one of those women who diets all the time, are you?'

'No sir,' I said. 'I could eat a horse.'

'I took the liberty of calling the coastguard earlier this morning,' Knox continued, as he tucked a linen napkin into his lap. 'The captain of the port said that you'd been reported missing and that your friends will meet you at the wharf when we dock.'

I wondered what friends he meant.

I'd kicked off my shoes while treading water in the Potomac, so I was still wearing my slippers with the seal of the Secretary of the Navy embroidered on their toes. I intended to keep them. When I walked down the plank arm in arm with Secretary Knox I found Major Wicker and Harvey Royal waiting for me. They both looked like they'd spent the night in a foxhole under machine-gun fire. I'm sure I looked worse.

I found myself in Royal's arms in tears while Wicker patted me awkwardly on the back.

Secretary Knox walked past me on his way to his car accompanied by an aide who'd met him at the dock. He smiled at me and touched his hat. I detached an arm from Royal's hug and waved back at Knox.

After the three of us collected ourselves we walked down the dock ourselves.

'I got out of the boat,' I began. 'The hatch door was locked. I thought I was going to drown.'

'You need sleep,' Wicker said. 'We all need sleep. We can talk later. Everything is under control.'

'Where is Clark? And Gachev? And Rose and Sadie? You have to tell me.'

'I'll drive her home and tell her everything,' Royal said.

'We must meet soon to debrief, though,' Wicker said. 'Over dinner tonight?'

'OK, if you're paying,' Royal said, handing me into his familiar Chevy police car.

On the way home Royal wasted no time telling me the worst of it. 'Clark is dead, Louise,' he said. 'Gachev killed him. They were meeting at a café and he shot him. We can't find Gachev either, he's gone underground.'

I swallowed hard. Poor Clark. His belief in a better future had blinded him to the truth about Stalin and the Soviet Union.

'What about Rose and Sadie?' I asked.

'They're in custody. But they told us everything, including all about the sailboat Clark had access to. And I found the taxi driver who took you to the wharf. But the coastguard couldn't search for you because of the weather. Thank God you're OK. How did you escape?'

I could not look that memory in the eye just yet.

'I can't talk about it now,' I said.

'Sure, no problem.'

Royal dropped me off at 'Two Trees'. Last night Wicker had had the presence of mind to get Rose to call Phoebe and tell her I was spending the night at her place. So no one at home would know what I had been through. I was glad of that.

No one was in the hallway. I slipped up the stairs and into my room. I found my 'Do Not Disturb' sign and hung it on my doorknob. My pajamas felt like the best silk imported from China, my sheets like the finest linen from India, and the Martini I fixed at ten in the morning tasted as delicious as the first one I ever had.

I fell deeply asleep.

*   *   *

I wanted no one at 'Two Trees' to know anything about what had happened to me over the last twenty-four hours. I told Phoebe and Ada that I'd had a swell sleepover at my friend's apartment playing bridge for hours, but that at work I'd developed a severe headache and come home to sleep it off. And I was going out to dinner tonight with more friends and would be home early.

'You've developed quite a social life,' Ada said. 'It's about time.'

Wicker picked me up in front of the Western Market in his big Studebaker. He was out of uniform and Royal was with him. Royal climbed out of the car and opened the passenger seat door for me.

Wicker pulled out into traffic.

'I've booked a private room at Ciro's,' Wicker said, 'where we can talk without being overheard.'

'Is that the red sauce joint on "G" Street?' asked Royal.

'Yeah,' Wicker said. 'You like Italian food?'

'Sure.'

'Louise, are you OK with Italian?' Wicker asked.

'I like spaghetti,' I said. 'That's all I've ever had.'

Our conversation seemed stupidly frivolous after all we had been through. I don't think we knew what to say to each other. This case was so complex we weren't aware of what each of us had done or what we each knew at any given time; even the timeline of events wasn't clear.

We weren't being debriefed at OSS so I supposed it would be up to Wicker to decide how much of this story would find its way into print and a Registry file. We weren't on our way to the police station either. Would Royal be permitted to arrest anyone for the crimes that had been committed? What would happen to me for my mistakes, starting with idiotically giving my real name to Hughes' landlady? I would be lucky if I only lost my Top Secret clearance.

The hostess showed us into a back room decorated like an Italian village. Stucco walls, tile-roofed canopies and puffy white clouds painted on the blue ceiling completed the design.

A waiter presented us with thick menus. Wicker pulled out a notebook and pen and laid them on the table.

'How big are your meatballs?' Royal asked the waiter.

'Golf balls,' the waiter said. 'Four to a serving.'

'Good, I don't like those little ones. That's what I'll have. And a beer.'

'Louise, would you like to share a pizza with me?' Wicker said. 'Have you had pizza yet?'

My stomach had contracted as soon as I saw Wicker pull out his pen and pad of paper.

My mistakes were about to be recorded for eternity. I doubted I could eat anything. No, I hadn't tasted pizza yet, but why not?

'Sure,' I said, 'I'll share a pizza with you.'

Wicker ordered us a Neapolitan pizza and beer.

We were all happy when the beers arrived.

'Let's begin,' Wicker said, opening up his pad.

We took turns telling our stories, beginning with Royal, then me and then Wicker. To say that all three of us learned things we hadn't known before was an understatement. For instance Wicker found out from Royal for the first time that Hughes' wallet had been found under a bench days after the murder. They agreed that it must have been planted. I told them that I'd seen Rose pack up Hughes' lighter, keys and pocketknife in the safe room. We agreed it made no sense for those items to be in Hughes' room. They should be in a man's pockets. I had a thought about that, but it hadn't gelled yet so I didn't mention it. And when I told the two men of my ordeal on the sailboat my voice broke several times and Royal reached over the basket of garlic bread to squeeze my hand.

'Mrs Pearlie,' Wicker said. 'This is a good time to reassure you that only a commendation will appear in your file.'

I couldn't believe it! I felt dizzy with relief.

'It would have been wise not to tell Mrs Nighy your real name, and you ought not to have run errands for Sergeant

Royal, but he has assured me you refused to give him any information that he wouldn't have been able to find out for himself if he had been allowed to pursue the Hughes murder case.'

'Thank you, Major Wicker,' I said. 'But I should have played along with Clark and Gachev when they asked me to join the spy ring. I was just so taken aback.'

'I put you in a situation for which you had no preparation,' Wicker said. 'That was my mistake. If you had died on that boat it would have been my responsibility.'

'Pardon me,' I said, 'I need to powder my nose.'

'Of course,' Wicker said. The two men stood as I left the table.

'You know,' Royal said to Wicker, 'if you send that girl back to the file room you'll be wasting her.'

'I agree,' Wicker said. 'I'm going to find another spot for her. I just don't know where yet.'

In the ladies' restroom I let my nerves stop twanging while I sponged the perspiration off my face and neck with paper towels. I still had my job! And a commendation to boot! And I didn't forget to powder my nose and apply lipstick before I went back to the table.

When I returned to the table our food had arrived and I found that I was hungry after all. The pizza was the prettiest pie I'd ever seen, and scrumptious too. Creamy yellow cheese, baked fresh tomatoes and an Italian sauce full of unfamiliar herbs layered the thick crust. I ate my half of the pie with gusto.

After the table was cleared the waiter brought us fresh Italian coffee. Royal ordered tiramisu for all of us. We waited until the waiter left before discussing the murder again.

'Conclusions?' Wicker asked.

'Lev Gachev killed Clark Leach and Paul Hughes and I can't arrest him for it,' Royal said grudgingly.

'Wait a minute,' I said. 'When did you decide that? Gachev didn't kill Paul Hughes!'

'Isn't it obvious?' Wicker said. 'Gachev was the "G" that Hughes met that Sunday night. I wonder if Hughes told Gachev that he wouldn't work for him anymore.'

'I don't know what Gachev and Hughes talked about at their meeting. But I know Gachev didn't kill him. Spencer Benton murdered Paul Hughes,' I said. The sound of my voice surprised me. My mind had just dropped the missing piece into the correct space in the puzzle that was Hughes' death. I had barely processed my conclusion myself when I spoke out.

'Hold on there,' Royal said. 'How do you figure that?'

We cut our conversation off as the waiter brought us our tiramisu. None of us touched it; we were too absorbed in our conversation.

'Do you have that grubby map you're always carrying around with you?' I asked Royal.

Royal withdrew the map from his pocket and handed it to me. I unfolded it and spread it out on the table.

'Clark Leach told me in the car on the way to the wharf that Gachev couldn't have killed Paul because the murder was the work of an amateur. Would Gachev have struck a man on the head in a public place, tossed his body in the water and, even worse, used his own return address on a fake telegram? Or come back to the scene days later to plant his wallet? I don't think so.'

I tapped the map right on the Tidal Basin.

'This is where everything happened. Sunday evening Paul was on his way back home from his meeting with "G" at his shop. He'd have taken a streetcar from the terminus, right here,' I said, pointing it out on the map. 'Spencer Benton was returning from a reception at the Capital Yacht Club here, about ten blocks east on the Washington Channel. The one his wife refused to attend with him. He'd still have been furious with her. We know from Rose that Spencer and Peggy had a huge fight that day. I wouldn't be surprised if Benton hit her – he was that kind of man – and Peggy is not a tough woman. I think Benton forced her to tell him about the affair, the spy ring and "G", even the location of "G"'s shop. And Benton knew that if OSS discovered all this it would ruin him.'

'After the reception at the Capital Yacht Club Benton also went to the terminus to catch a streetcar. He and Paul ran into each other. They walked along the Tidal Basin path together toward the streetcar stop.'

'They may have stopped to have a drink somewhere,' Royal said, 'the medical examiner found alcohol in Hughes' blood.'

'Paul didn't know that Benton had learned about the spy ring and his affair with Peggy. He turned his back on Benton, who then smashed Hughes' skull with a rock,' I said. 'He emptied Hughes' pockets to delay his identification and dumped his body into the Basin. Then he walked a couple of blocks to the nearest Western Union office and sent a telegram, using Gachev's shop as the return address to incriminate him.'

'Why would he do that?' Royal asked. 'Wouldn't Gachev tell all if he were arrested? Reveal that Peggy and the others were spying for him?'

'No,' Wicker said. 'Gachev would never reveal anything about the spy ring. Not ever. Besides, he would disappear before we could arrest him. As he has.'

'But you don't have any real evidence that Benton knew any of this,' Royal said.

'I think he did. Benton is a tyrant who wanted complete control over his wife. He tried to prevent her from having a social life of her own. He asked me to convince Peggy to stay away from Rose and Sadie because they were bad influences on her. She was devastated after Paul's death. Cried in public over him. Benton must have bullied Peggy until she told him everything.'

'You have no proof that Benton planted the wallet,' Wicker said.

'I don't,' I said, 'but I know who planted the other items from Hughes' pocket in the safe room.'

'Who?' both men said.

'Peggy Benton was the first of the group to go into the residential hotel. She had plenty of time to plant the lighter, the pocketknife and the keys. To strengthen the deception that

Hughes' pockets hadn't been intentionally stripped. That he'd dropped his wallet and left the other items in the safe room,' I said.

'She knew that her husband killed Paul,' Royal said. 'Maybe Spencer told her.'

'Or she found the wallet and other things where Spencer had hidden them,' Wicker said. 'Or Spencer may have kept them to torment her.'

'No matter how much she loved Hughes it would ruin her life if Spencer was arrested. She tried to protect him. Did she plant the wallet too?'

'I don't know,' I said. 'Maybe Spencer did.'

'Hold on now, we're just speculating,' Royal said. 'Where are the Bentons now?'

'Confined to their apartment,' Wicker said.

'If you could get Peggy alone she would confess to everything, I know she would,' I said to Royal.

Royal picked up his fork and shoveled tiramisu into his mouth. Then he pulled a napkin out of his pocket and wrapped up the rest of the dessert, tucking it back into his pocket.

'I'm on my way over to the Bentons',' Royal said, pushing his chair back. 'That is, if the big shots have no objection.'

'None,' Wicker said, 'as long as you can think of a way to keep OSS out of it.'

'We'll make a deal with Benton. A life sentence instead of execution for murdering his wife's lover as long as he doesn't mention the espionage ring. He'll take it.'

'What will happen to Sadie, Rose and Peggy?' I asked.

Wicker shrugged. 'We'll dismiss them from OSS, of course. But other than that, nothing. With Gachev gone we have no corroborating evidence. They were just pawns anyway.'

On his way out of the room Royal patted me on the shoulder awkwardly.

'I'm so glad you're all right, Louise. I would never have forgiven myself if something had happened to you.'

I gripped his hand. 'After you retire, call me and we'll celebrate.'

'I'll do that,' he said, and left the room.

Wicker and I finished our dessert and coffee. The tiramisu was grand! I wondered if I could make it myself.

As we prepared to leave the restaurant Wicker turned to me. 'Mrs Pearlie, I'm giving you a few days' leave. You need some rest.'

The next day I caught the three thirty train from Union Station to Grand Central Station in New York City. Joe would be waiting for me there.

AFTERWORD

William Franklin 'Frank' Knox (January 1, 1874–April 28, 1944) was an American newspaper editor and publisher. He was also the Republican vice-presidential candidate in 1936 and Secretary of the Navy under Franklin D. Roosevelt during most of World War II.

Although Knox was a Republican he favored early intervention in the war in Europe, and was a key connection between Roosevelt and the isolationist Republicans, who were in the majority of their party before Pearl Harbor.

FDR wasn't the first Roosevelt Knox worked for. He was a 'Rough Rider' in Cuba with Teddy Roosevelt.

Knox was also my great-great-uncle. Of course I run across him often during my research, and I've been looking for an opportunity for him to make a cameo appearance in one of my books. I think offering Louise refuge on the *Sequoia* after her ordeal on the Potomac was a good choice!

Thanks, Uncle Frank, for your service to your country. Your family is proud of you.

Sarah Shaber

Lightning Source UK Ltd.
Milton Keynes UK
UKOW01f1423020317
295719UK00001B/30/P